And then he did it. He pulled her into his arms, and she gasped slightly just before his lips came down on hers. Even as he started to kiss her, he wasn't sure what he was doing. There was just so much fire between them and this was the only thing that would quench it.

Gabrielle stiffened in his arms, a moan of protest escaping her lips. But as he slipped his arms around her slim waist and pulled her against his body, he felt the moment when she surrendered to the kiss.

She softened against him, and Lord, all of the tension ebbed out of Omar's body. This was how he wanted her. Her lips and body pressed against his. As she kissed him back, the woman who seemed only able to fight with him morphed into someone else. She was blossoming into—

Gabrielle violently pushed herself out of his arms. As she looked up at him, her eyes shot fire. "What the heck are you doing?" she demanded.

"Kissing you."

"I know that. But, my God, why?"

"Seemed like the most effective way to quiet you," Omar muttered. He wasn't surprised when her eyes widened with fury.

Dear Reader,

Sometimes it's tough being a romance writer. Imagining all those hot heroes and sexy scenes? Delving into a world where that sexy hero becomes putty in the right woman's hands? It's hard work!

Of course, I'm kidding. Not about writing being hard work, but it's certainly the *best* work for the very reasons I mentioned above. What's better than writing about a hot hero and a feisty heroine who meet and there's instant fire?

That's exactly what happens in *Passion Ignited*. Literally, sparks fly between Omar and Gabrielle because they're at a fire scene. And also figuratively, because the heat between them is immediate.

I know how much you love continuing stories—*and* a playboy hero who doesn't want to settle down. That's why this book is about Omar, who you may recognize from the first two books in my Love on Fire series. Little does Omar know, his playboy days are numbered! This was a fun story to write, and I hope you all love it!

Kayla

Passion IGNITED

Kayla Perrin

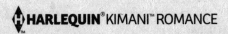

HARLEQUIN® KIMANI™ ROMANCE

Recycling programs
for this product may
not exist in your area.

ISBN-13: 978-0-373-86418-8

Passion Ignited

Copyright © 2015 by Kayla Perrin

For questions and comments about the quality of this book please contact us
at CustomerService@Harlequin.com.

Printed in U.S.A.

www.Harlequin.com

Kayla Perrin is a multi-award winning, multi-published *USA TODAY* and *Essence* bestselling author. She's been writing since she could hold a pencil and sent her first book to a publisher when she was just thirteen years old. Since 1998, she's had over fifty novels and novellas published. She's been featured in *Ebony*, *RT Book Reviews*, *South Florida Business Journal*, the *Toronto Star* and other Canadian and US publications. Her works have been translated into Italian, German, Spanish and Portuguese. In 2011, Kayla received the prestigious Harry Jerome Award for excellence in the arts in Canada. She lives in the Toronto area with her daughter.

You can find Kayla on Facebook, Twitter and Instagram. Please visit her website at kaylaperrin.com.

Books by Kayla Perrin

Harlequin Kimani Romance

Island Fantasy
Freefall to Desire
Taste of Desire
Always in My Heart
Surrender My Heart
Heart to Heart
Until Now
Burning Desire
Flames of Passion
Passion Ignited

Visit the Author Profile page at Harlequin.com for more titles.

For Chloe,
my beautiful and talented daughter.
Your drive and artistic ability
inspire me everyday.
Never give up on your dreams!
I can't wait to see how high your star rises.

Chapter 1

The somber rendition of "Going Home" filled the air, played as it always was, by the bagpipe and drum band. The rhythmic sound of dress boots hitting the asphalt in unison accompanied the sound of the music. Firefighters from all of Ocean City's fire departments marched in formation, following the ladder truck that carried Dean Dunbar's flag-draped coffin.

Omar Ewing hated the sound of the pipe and drum band. Hated it with a passion. Besides the rare happy occasions—like Saint Patrick's Day celebrations—this type of music always signified a funeral.

Firefighters from well beyond Ocean City's borders in California—even from outside the country—lined the streets for the procession. Police officers and paramedics were among the crowd, too. The case of the Ocean City arsonist had garnered international attention and the turnout to pay final respects to Lt. Dean Dunbar was impressive.

It was exactly as Lt. Omar Ewing knew it would be. Firefighters and other first responders always supported each other when someone was killed in the line of duty. If it was feasible, they traveled as far as they could to attend the funeral of a fallen brother or sister.

This was no exception.

The procession approached the spot where two fire trucks were on opposite sides of the street, their ladders extended on an angle toward each other. Held up by the ladders was a giant American flag. This was a day to remember Dean's sacrifice. People were proud of his sacrifice. But all Omar could think about was that it shouldn't have happened.

He and the rest of his brothers knew the risks of the job they did, of course. But that didn't make it any easier.

Cameras flashed, video cameras rolled. This story would be on every news station and in newspapers across the country.

A huge number of civilians had come out. They stood on both sides of the road, many waving American flags. A good firefighter had fallen. Dean Dunbar had just been doing his job, protecting the citizens of Ocean City by battling a blaze that had threatened an entire neighborhood. The fire at a meat packaging company had been a monster. Several other firefighters had sustained injuries. All because some sicko was out there taking pleasure in wreaking havoc on the city.

Omar glanced up at the sky. It was bright and sunny, without even a cloud. It seemed illogical that it was such a beautiful day when he and his colleagues were mourning the loss of a fallen brother.

Dean Dunbar had been a firefighter for twenty-two years. His wife and two teenage boys were absolutely devastated. It was hard to see them so grief stricken. His wife in particular was barely able to contain herself. Her two sons were helping hold her upright.

He should have been able to retire and enjoy his family after putting in so many years with the fire department.

But nothing was guaranteed. Not in life, and especially when your job involved putting your life on the line.

Omar knew the risks, but he would have it no other way. For him, saving a life was the ultimate reward. There was no better feeling than knowing he could save someone. It was the reason that he and his fellow firefighters did this dangerous job.

The procession arrived at the church. Dunbar's widow began to sob as the pallbearers took the coffin from the top of the fire truck. The bagpipe and drums continued to play.

Omar scanned the faces in the crowd. Was the arsonist there? Was he watching with a sense of smug satisfaction?

Omar could only look around briefly before continuing into the church, where he and all the mourners would pay their final respects to Lt. Dean Dunbar.

Hours later, many of the Ocean City firefighters were packed into a bar. They had come to raise a glass for Dean Dunbar, something they did after every funeral. Omar knew that Dean would want it no other way.

Omar, Mason and a few more of the men from Fire Station Two were sitting at the far end of the bar. There was faint laughter as people remembered Dean fondly. But there was also a lot of sadness and anger.

"We have to catch this guy," Omar said.

"Absolutely," Mason agreed. "This has gone on long enough. Now we've lost one of our own."

Omar took a pull of his beer. "Somebody, somewhere knows who this guy is. A girlfriend, a sibling."

"We'll get him," Mason said. "We have to."

"I have a bad feeling that the arsonist is going to ramp up his game," Omar commented. "I'll bet he was in the crowd, watching the procession. Probably got a kick out of seeing the family grieving."

"There are a lot of deranged people out there," Paul, another firefighter from their station, said. "Now that someone has died, hopefully everyone will be vigilant. Anything suspicious, people need to report. Whether that's on the street, or at home. I don't want to lose another firefighter. And definitely not a civilian."

Omar raised his beer. "For Dean Dunbar."

Mason, Paul and the firefighters within earshot raised their glasses. "For Dean Dunbar," they said in unison.

As Omar drank, he knew there was one other thing they could do to honor Dean's memory. And that was to find the arsonist.

Hopefully before he struck again.

Surprisingly—and thankfully—there were no fires over the Christmas holiday. People had gone from being fearful and waiting for the other shoe to drop, to feeling hopeful again. Maybe the arsonist had suddenly gotten a conscience. Maybe he'd gotten bored with setting fires. Or maybe he had moved away.

Whatever the reason, the air seemed clearer in Ocean City, and the sun brighter. People were living their lives again. Until the first week of January when the arsonist struck again. A Chinese restaurant was set ablaze just after midnight.

Tom Sully, the fire chief at Station Two, was on the scene, giving orders. "Ewing, Williams. Get that ladder to the roof so we attack the fire from there. Roman, DeNiro—get a hose to the back of the building. Duff,

Riley—you two attack it from the front. The restaurant closed at ten, thank God, so there's no one inside. Let's kill this thing—fast!"

A small crowd had gathered on the sidewalk. People stared from the high-rise across the street, looking down undoubtedly with horror at the chaos. But had anyone seen the arsonist?

"When are you going to catch the jerk?" someone yelled.

"How long do we have to live in fear?"

Omar and his fellow firefighters set about fighting the fire. Even if they had time to answer the questions being asked, they would be unable to do so because they didn't have the answers.

Omar was as determined to see this arsonist caught as anyone else. The fires needed to stop—and the sooner, the better.

As Omar climbed the ladder to go onto the top of the building, fire exploded through a window. Instinctively, he lurched backward. People below him screamed.

His heart pounding, Omar regained his footing and continued up the ladder. This would be yet another building lost. By the time they had arrived, the entire structure was on fire. Whoever was behind this knew just how to operate under the cover of darkness so that the response of any fire station would be too late to stop the most damage.

Omar glanced over his shoulder as he neared the top of the building. Despite the late hour, the crowd had grown.

Was the arsonist among them, watching them at this very minute?

It took a good hour to put out the fire. In that time, the crowd had continued to grow instead of wane. Omar could hear the angry rants among the spectators. People were tired of their city being under attack. People wanted the arsonist apprehended immediately.

Omar went over to Tyler McKenzie, the engineer on the pump truck. He was spraying water from the nozzle of a hose, allowing firefighters to drink and cool down. Naturally, fires were hot. But add to that, the protective gear they had to wear, and they all were sweating profusely underneath.

"Omar, drink," Tyler said.

Omar put his face beneath the spray of water, sighing as the cold water splashed his hot face. Then he angled his head to drink several gulps.

As he stepped away from the hose, his eyes were on the crowd. Suddenly, he spotted a face that gave him pause. It was a woman wearing a baseball cap pulled low over the top of her head.

A black baseball cap.

He had seen her before…at the last fire. He was sure of it.

He watched her. Unlike the other spectators, she wasn't checking out the scene before her. She seemed fidgety, her head turned to the right. Had she seen Omar looking at her, and was now avoiding making eye contact?

Suddenly, she started to move. She weaved her way through the crowd, walking briskly.

Omar started after her.

"Ewing," Chief Sully called.

"Chief, I think I saw something."

"What?" the chief asked.

But Omar didn't have time to answer. He only had time to give chase. He made his way along the street in front of the crowd of onlookers, vaguely aware that they were observing him with curiosity.

Someone gasped as he pushed his way into the crowd. "Excuse me," he said. "Sorry." And kept going.

He saw the woman—dressed in dark colors—round the corner into an alley. Omar started to jog. As he got to the opening of the alley, he saw her running.

She was clearly trying to get away.

"You've got to be kidding me," Omar muttered. A woman? A woman was the one setting the fires in Ocean City?

That was the only thing that explained why she would be running after he had picked her out of the crowd.

He started to run faster. With his long legs, he caught up to her in no time. "Stop right there!" he yelled.

The woman didn't stop, just glanced over her shoulder at him before turning sharply to the right.

Omar picked up speed, darting around the corner she had just taken. He saw her heading toward Clark Street. Within seconds, he was upon her again. He reached out and grabbed her by the arm, and whipped her around. As he pulled her toward him, she landed against his body.

She looked up at him, her eyes flaming.

"What are you doing?" she demanded.

"What are *you* doing?" he countered.

"I was chasing the arsonist!"

"Funny," Omar said wryly. "That's exactly what I was going to say."

She looked at him, aghast. "What?"

"I saw you. And you saw that I saw you in the crowd. Then you took off."

Her eyes widened with indignation as she forced her body away from his. "Didn't you see that guy?"

"Right, lady. The only person I saw was you. Looking suspicious in the crowd, then taking off." Omar tightened his hand on her upper arm. He wasn't about to let her go.

"The whole city's been waiting for this day. I've got to admit, I didn't expect the person terrorizing Ocean City to be a woman."

"You must be out of your mind."

"*I'm* the one out of my mind?" Omar retorted.

"I'm not the arsonist!"

"You can tell your story to the police." Omar started walking with her toward Clark Street, but she dug her heels into the ground and tried to yank her arm free.

"Let me go!" she demanded.

"I don't think so."

"You're making a mistake."

"Sure I am."

When Omar continued to drag her toward Clark Street, she groaned, and then said, "Why am I not surprised? No one in this town is doing their job to catch the arsonist."

"Nice try."

With her free hand, she whipped off her baseball cap. Her dark shoulder-length hair spilled free. Omar's immediate thought was how beautiful she was. He could see her face fully now beneath the streetlights. What would drive a woman like her to commit such heinous crimes?

"You don't recognize me?"

Omar shrugged. Wait... He hadn't dated her in the past, had he?

No. He would remember her.

He saw a look flash on her face. It was subtle. Disappointment? Perhaps a little surprise? He wasn't sure.

"I'm not who you think I am," she said. She craned her neck to look around the corner onto Clark Street, and then threw up a hand in frustration. "And my God, you just let the arsonist get away."

The sound of exasperation in her tone caused Omar to halt. Was she actually telling the truth?

"Why are you out here dressed in dark colors?" Omar asked. "And why did you run when you saw me?"

"I didn't run when I saw you," she quipped. "I ran because I was certain I saw the arsonist."

Frowning, Omar released her. "You were serious about that?"

"Yes!"

"Who are you? And why are you out here alone trying to take down the arsonist?"

"Because *someone* has to." She let out a frustrated breath, then reached into the pocket of her jacket. "I'm Gabrielle Leonard. I thought you might recognize me when I took my hat off, but you probably don't watch community television."

Omar said nothing.

"Anyway," she continued. "I'm a producer and host at Cable Four. I have a very successful show. *Your Hour*—"

"Ahh," Omar interjected, finally understanding. "So you're a reporter, out here trying to get a scoop."

"This isn't about a scoop," she said. "This is about catching the person who—as you said—has been terrorizing our city. But thanks to you, he just got away."

Her eyes shot fire as she studied him, yet all Omar could think was how attractive she looked. Was she always this heated?

He kept a level head as he said, "You're a reporter. Not a cop. If you had pertinent information, you should have given it to the authorities." Now Omar was beginning to get irritated. All too often reporters got in the way—because they wanted to get the almighty story. "You were in the crowd. You looked suspicious. And that's why I came after you. I hope to God the person you saw wasn't actually the arsonist." His eyes roamed over her body. She was all of five foot five, maybe a hundred and ten pounds.

"How exactly were you planning to take him down? By batting your eyelashes?"

"Oh, that's priceless. Now you're going to throw out sexist insults?"

"You're a reporter, not a cop."

"I'm a TV host and producer."

"Whatever. The last thing we need is a civilian inserting herself into the investigation."

"Someone's got to catch this guy," Gabrielle muttered.

"Yeah—the professionals."

"Fine. He's long gone, anyway." She glared at him, as if to emphasize that it was his fault. "Now that I've been duly lectured by you, I'll take it into consideration for when the next fire happens."

Oh, she had a mouth on her. Both literally and figuratively. Her full lips looked sweet. Yet she spewed such sarcasm and sourness. Why was she treating him like the enemy?

"Goodbye." She turned in the direction of Clark Street. But Omar put a hand on her shoulder, stopping her.

She turned, looking up at him in surprise.

Omar said, "Not so fast."

Chapter 2

Gabrielle's eyes widened as she looked at the firefighter. Why was he stopping her *now*?

"Don't tell me you still don't believe me," she said.

"I do…believe you."

"Then why aren't you letting me go?"

He didn't speak for a moment, and she noticed the way he was suddenly looking at her. There was something in his eyes. It was a look that Gabrielle had seen many a time. Most notably, with her own ex-fiancé—when he had leveled his eyes on other women.

This man was a player. It was practically written on his forehead. So often, the attractive ones were.

"If you are out here hoping to get a scoop, I have to ask that you don't insert yourself into this investigation. Things get complicated when journalists get in the way."

Gabrielle gritted her teeth, and held back a nasty retort. Of course, he didn't believe her. He clearly thought she was interested in nabbing the arsonist for the glory. But that had nothing to do with it. She was in this for justice.

Justice for her parents.

Her parents had been victims of the arsonist. Their restaurant—the culmination of their hopes and dreams—had been burned down after only six months in operation. Two weeks later, her father had had a heart attack. The stress had gotten to him, and he'd almost died.

"I'm trying to catch this arsonist, because somebody has to. He has the city gripped with fear, and it's mind-boggling that no one is able to figure out who he is and stop him."

"You don't think we're doing our job?"

"Not good enough," Gabrielle said.

She saw a little bit of irritation flash in the firefighter's eyes. And she wondered why she was goading him. They shouldn't be at odds. Ultimately they had the same goal. Yet, they were arguing.

"Why don't you have a camera crew with you?" Omar suddenly asked.

The question caught her off guard. She wasn't prepared for it. "I'm not here in an official capacity with the station. I already told you, this isn't about me getting a story."

"But you were at the last fire. Maybe the one before that, too. I've seen you before. That's why, when I saw you tonight, I thought it was suspicious. More than a co-incidence."

"It is more than a coincidence. I heard about the fire on the radio, and I came down to the scene. Same as I did with the last fire. You guys are busy, and I wanted to see if I spotted anyone in the crowd who looked suspicious. I came armed with my cell phone camera."

"You got the arsonist on camera? Why didn't you say so?"

"You see how dark it is out here. I got pictures, but they're not great. And I couldn't get close to the guy."

"Can you give me a description of him?"

"Not exactly."

Omar chuckled mercilessly. "But you were so certain that you were chasing the right guy. This is ridiculous."

The only thing ridiculous was that he was paying no attention to her at all. He wasn't getting it.

"I couldn't tell who he was because I wasn't right beside him. And because he also was wearing a hat. And it's dark out. I can tell you that he's a white male. I saw him at the last fire as well. When I saw him tonight… I just knew."

"Then why didn't you try to get the attention of someone in authority?" Omar asked.

"I…" She had been too absorbed with trying to keep her eye on the person she believed to be the arsonist. "I'm not sure it would have done any good. The authorities in the city seem completely inept at catching this perp."

"Ouch." Omar made a face. "For such a beautiful lady, you certainly know how to hurt a guy's feelings."

Then he smiled. And Gabrielle's jaw went slack. She couldn't believe it. He was flirting with her!

"Omar!"

The firefighter turned. Another firefighter—Gabrielle recognized Mason Foley, because he had been in the papers some months earlier—was striding toward them through the alley. "Did you find something?"

"Thought I did," Omar answered. "But I was wrong, apparently."

Mason's eyes narrowed on Gabrielle. "Her?"

"I saw her in the crowd," Omar explained. "She was acting suspicious. I saw her take off, so I did too. When

I caught up to her, she said she was in pursuit of the al-
leged arsonist."

"Until he got in the way and stopped me," Gabrielle
quipped.

"You're Gabrielle Leonard, aren't you?" Mason asked.

"Yes." At least this guy didn't only read the sports
pages, she thought sourly.

"The guy got away," Omar said. "Did you see anyone
running down Clark Street?"

Mason shook his head. "Naw."

"Damn."

Gabrielle looked up at Omar. There was something
about him that looked familiar. And his name…

Yes! It came to her. Hadn't he dated a friend of a
friend? Two, from what she remembered. Both had been
head over heels for Omar, but he'd broken their hearts.
There was some story about a love triangle. It had been a
few years back. But it was becoming clearer in her mind.
Omar had played both the women. In the end, both had
been devastated.

"Omar, we need you back at the truck," Mason said.

Omar suddenly met her gaze. And there was that look
again. Now Gabrielle could define it. It was the bedroom
eye. She quickly averted her gaze to Mason, who nodded
at her, and said, "Have a good day."

Then she looked at Omar again, and though it was a
quick glance, she felt something she didn't want to feel.
A spark of attraction. There was an undeniable sizzle between the two of them.

She jerked her gaze away and turned down the alley.

"Gabrielle," Omar called.

But she pretended not to hear. Because the last thing she
wanted to do was have any further involvement with him.

* * *

"Don't quit your day job," Tyler McKenzie joked when all of the firefighters had returned to Station Two. "You'd make a lousy detective, Omar."

The guys had a good laugh at Omar's expense. Mason, having gotten a kick out of the fact that Omar had "nabbed" Gabrielle Leonard, had enthusiastically shared the story. With everyone.

"Very funny, Tyler," Omar said.

"Wasn't Stacy Jackson out there with Channel 10 news?" Mason asked. "Maybe she's the arsonist."

More raucous laughter from the guys.

Omar rolled his eyes. Okay, so he had made a colossal mistake. Gabrielle Leonard was clearly not the arsonist.

"I couldn't see her face," Omar said. "She was wearing a hat." Though he wouldn't have recognized her even in the light of day. He never tuned in to to any Cable Four programming.

"Surprising," Tyler said. "You mean there's actually a woman in Ocean City you *don't* recognize? I thought you've dated all of them."

"You keep that up, you won't make it to your wedding," Omar warned him.

Tyler had recently gotten engaged—for the second time. His first engagement had been a mistake, something Omar and the other guys at the station had known almost from the beginning. But Tyler had hung on far longer than he should have, trying to make things work. It had been futile.

But a few months ago, Tyler had met someone else. Their connection had been wild and furious, and now he seemed happier than ever.

Omar had felt an instant connection to Gabrielle, as

well. Sure, she was beautiful. That was obvious. But it wasn't simply her beauty. There was something else. There had to be—because she had been undeniably angry with him, yet he still felt a spark.

"What was some woman from a TV station doing at the fire scene anyway?" Omar asked.

"She's not just some woman," Mason said. "She's Gabrielle Leonard. A local celebrity."

"Yeah well, I never watch community television."

"We don't even want to know what stations you watch!" Tyler said, then laughed.

"You're a regular comedian today," Omar said to Tyler. "I don't have to watch it, when I can be out there living it."

There was a round of ooohs and enthusiastic laughter. Someone patted him on the back, and said, "Our resident stud."

Omar chuckled. His reputation at the station was one of a ladies' man. And it was true, he had dated a lot. But he hadn't dated seriously, at least not in recent years. For that reason, the guys all thought he wasn't serious about finding a girlfriend.

It wasn't that he wasn't serious about it. He just hadn't met anyone who had really intrigued him. Oh, he'd met plenty of beautiful women. And he dated many of them. But they all failed to interest him past the initial attraction. So what was he supposed to do? Settle?

"That's our Omar," one of the paramedics said. She was female, and she liked to tease Omar for his playboy ways.

It wasn't that he was simply a playboy. At least, that's not how he set out to live his life. And he knew he wasn't getting any younger. He was thirty-six. Like practically the rest of society, the idea of settling down and having a family was one that appealed to him. But he first had to find the right woman.

Omar knew that if he told his colleagues at the station that, they would break into spontaneous laughter. He had to take responsibility for his own reputation, but part of his carefree attitude had been an act. He didn't talk about it, but Omar had lost the love of his life. Losing Mika had devastated him. And since her death, he hadn't met anyone else who could compare.

His mind went back to Gabrielle. He'd felt something with her in that alley. Something he wanted to explore.

The problem was, she had walked away from him when he had called out. She'd ignored him, making it clear that she wanted nothing more to do with him.

Well, Omar would see about that. One way or another.

"What are you doing?" Gabrielle asked.

Omar pulled her toward his body, and looked down into her eyes as if trying to claim her with his gaze. "Kissing you."

He began to lower his lips slowly, and just when his lips touched hers, Gabrielle felt her body explode.

Her eyes popped open. For a moment, Gabrielle didn't know what was going on. Her heart was beating fast. She was in her bed, she soon realized. Which meant…

Which meant she had been dreaming about Omar.

Dear God in heaven, what was wrong with her? She glanced at the clock. It was just after four in the morning, and she needed to be up in a few hours. Yet, she had been sleeping fitfully. For some reason, her mind wouldn't stop replaying what had happened the previous night. How she had been running down that alley, then suddenly stopped by Omar. How the perp had gotten away.

The smoldering look Omar had given her…

Sitting up in the bed, she reached for her water bottle on the night table. She knew why she kept replaying what had happened. And it was because she had been so close to nailing the arsonist.

Did she look like a crazy person? The fact that Omar actually believed she had been the arsonist was baffling.

As she sipped from a glass of water at her bedside, she conceded that perhaps she *had* looked fidgety and suspicious. She had been keeping one eye on the fire, and one eye on the person she thought had started it. She didn't want to get too close and scare him off. But she had tried—surreptitiously—to get photos of him.

She wasn't sure if she had spooked him, but suddenly he had started to move out of the crowd. Toward the alley. There had been no time to try to get anyone else's attention. Gabrielle had done the only thing she could do. Follow him.

How exactly were you planning to take him down? By batting your eyelashes?

The firefighter's sarcastic question sounded in her mind. Would he have asked her that had she been a male civilian? Or would he have applauded a male for a valiant effort to take down a wanted criminal?

Gabrielle lay back down on the bed and snuggled with her pillow. Again, she thought about the look Omar had given her just before they parted. It irked her all the more to know that they had been talking about something serious, and then he had given her the bedroom eye. As though all she was good for was something sexual.

Of course, Gabrielle was jumping to conclusions. He hadn't said anything inappropriate. Well, except for that one sexist comment. He certainly hadn't crossed the line with her. But…

It was that spark she had felt. Amidst their arguing,

she had felt a pull of attraction. Which made her wonder if she were losing her mind.

She looked at the pillow beside her. The empty pillow. The pillow where her ex-fiancé used to sleep.

Until he had cheated on her.

Maybe that was what was bothering her about the encounter with Omar. Besides the disturbing fact that he let the perp get away, maybe she had seen in him the very qualities she used to see in Tobias.

Yes… That was it. She had sensed in him the same kind of philandering ways she had sensed in Tobias. That's why she had gotten angry with him.

Tobias Winthrop. What a joke. He'd had such a sophisticated name, and he'd had the pedigree to go along with it. Firstborn child of a wealthy businessman. Tobias began working at his father's company even while in college. From that point, he was groomed to become the CEO of Winthrop Publishing. He had talked about how wonderful their future would be, how they could be a power couple in Ocean City. How they could sail the seas on a private yacht and take private planes to exotic destinations.

He had swept Gabrielle off her feet. But all the money in the world couldn't buy happiness. She had learned that the hard way when Tobias had cheated on her with her own cousin.

Gabrielle rolled over in her bed and tightly shut her eyes. Why was she thinking about Tobias and his betrayal?

She knew why. It was her brain's way of reminding her that men like Tobias—and Omar—were dangerous to her heart. She had felt a spark of attraction for Omar. And now, her brain was screaming at her with all kinds of signals. Trying to remind her that even being attracted to someone like Omar could lead to heartbreak.

"Good grief," she said to herself. "Why are you even getting yourself worked up over this?"

It wasn't as if she was going to see Omar again.

Chapter 3

The next day, Gabrielle felt exhausted at work. She hadn't had nearly enough sleep. But in her line of work, napping on the job was impossible. She'd had people to call and interview before appearances on the various shows that Cable Four produced. And she'd had to film her own show, *Your Hour*, and be upbeat while she was on air.

So she had done what she'd had to do. This had been a three-espresso day.

She didn't particularly like the strong drink. In fact, she consumed it more as if it were medicine. A liquid shot of adrenaline. It gave her an extra jolt when she was beginning to get fatigued. It allowed her to get through her day.

And when she was finished and finally leaving the studio, she wanted nothing more than to head home and get in her bed. But she couldn't. Not yet. She needed to visit her parents. Ever since her father's heart attack, she stopped by often to see how he was doing and to help cheer her mother up.

Gabrielle rounded the studio building to the parking lot…then stopped up dead in her tracks. Was that Omar?

It took only a second for her to realize that it was. And the nerve of him. He was leaning his butt against her Mercedes!

She hustled forward. As she did, he stood tall. He was six foot one at least. And now, in the daylight, without his firefighting gear, she could take a better look at him.

He had a medium brown complexion. He had a round face, which was both sexy and boyish at the same time. He was clean-shaven, and had closely cropped hair. And his body…his biceps were exposed beneath his shirt, and she could see the defined muscles, even though he wasn't flexing.

He was one seriously sexy man.

As Gabrielle got closer to him, she saw that he had a gold stud in his left earlobe. *Figures*, she thought. Was that on page one of the player's handbook?

"Gabby," Omar said, and gestured to her personalized license plate. "Figured this had to be yours."

Would it be completely rude to simply get into her car and drive away? Why Omar was even here, Gabrielle had no clue.

She pressed her electronic key to unlock her doors. "What are you going to do?" Omar asked. "Take off without talking to me?"

"How can I help you?"

"So formal."

Gabrielle crossed her arms over her chest. "Why are you here?"

"I wanted to talk to you about last night."

"I thought we discussed everything we needed to," Gabrielle said.

"I'm not sure why we've gotten off on the wrong foot," Omar began. "But there's a negative energy between us. I'd like to resolve that." He extended his hand to her, and offered her a charming smile. "Omar Ewing. Lieutenant at Fire Station Two. Pleased to meet you."

Gabrielle shook his hand. "Gabrielle Leonard."

"I realize you were upset because I judged you wrongly," Omar said. "And for that, I'm sorry."

"Apology accepted." She started toward her driver's side door.

"Whoa, wait a second." When Gabrielle turned to look over her shoulder at Omar, he said, "That's it? You're taking off?"

"I… I have an appointment." Not that it couldn't wait. But being near Omar caused her heart to beat quickly, and she was feeling suddenly flustered.

"All right. I'll be quick. You said you got a look at the guy you think is the arsonist. So I'm thinking it would be a good idea for the two of us to meet so that we can discuss whatever else it is that you've learned. Perhaps combined with what the arson investigators know, we might be able to finally take this guy down."

"All right," Gabrielle said slowly. "I'll give you my card. You can call my assistant tomorrow. Make an appointment."

Omar chuckled softly. "Call your assistant? I was thinking more like we could go to dinner."

Now Gabrielle was the one to laugh. Finally, she understood. "So you're here to ask me on a date?"

"A working date, if you will."

Predictable… He wanted another notch on his bedpost, and he had set his eyes on her.

"You can pick the place," Omar said. "We could do this tomorrow, if you want."

"Mr. Ewing. I wasn't born yesterday."

He made a face. "Excuse me?"

"I know what you really want."

Omar folded his arms over his brawny chest, and his biceps grew exponentially. He looked at her through narrowed eyes. "Really? What do I want?"

"Dinner?" Gabrielle scowled. "Does that work with all the women you hit on?"

His eyes widened. "You think I'm hitting on you?"

The way he said the words caused her jaw to stiffen a little. Though the reason was beyond her. She shouldn't be offended if he wasn't actually hitting on her. Because she didn't *want* him to hit on her.

And yet there was this itty-bitty feeling in the pit of her stomach that felt like rejection.

Or maybe it was just humiliation. Was she jumping to conclusions where Omar was concerned? Just like he had with her last night?

"If you really want to discuss the case, we can do it at my office."

"But dinner would be so much nicer."

Gabrielle knew his game. And just seeing him here had her unsettled. Her heart was still beating fast, and she had this odd sensation coursing through her body.

She didn't like it.

All she knew was that if she never saw Omar again, that would be the best thing for her.

"If I recall, you mentioned something yesterday about how I should go to the police with whatever I knew," she said. "I think that makes the most sense."

"Or, you and I could discuss what you think you know, then I can advise you on whether or not we should go to the police with it. I am a firefighter. I'm not some schmuck off the street."

No, he certainly wasn't. He was six foot one or so of hot black man. And that was the exact problem with him. Gabrielle could totally see herself losing focus around him. Because for the first time since Tobias had left her, she was feeling a stirring in her gut.

And that was the last thing she wanted. Especially with a man like Omar Ewing.

"I didn't say you were a schmuck."

"Sorry," Omar said, offering her a smile. "Just trying to lighten the mood."

"I really do have to get going." Gabrielle was hoping that she could slip away before he realized that she hadn't actually agreed to a date with him.

"You know what I really don't understand," Omar began. "Why you were at the scene of the fire hoping to nab the arsonist without any help from anyone at your cable station. The more I thought about it, it made more sense for you to go to the scene with someone who had a camera. You might have been able to get the suspected arsonist on film without him knowing."

"When I heard about the fire, it was late," Gabrielle explained. "Far too late to wake up any of our cameramen. So I just went to the scene of the fire on my own."

"What about someone else? A friend or boyfriend or husband who could have been there with you." He paused. "Didn't it occur to you that trying to go after the arsonist on your own could be dangerous?"

She almost laughed. He had thrown in *boyfriend or husband*, hoping to have her reveal her marital status. He thought he was smooth.

"Gabrielle?" Omar prompted when she didn't speak.

"I…" Gabrielle began, but her voice trailed off. How

could she answer that? She hadn't even discussed her plans with anyone from the network. She hadn't been at the fire scene in any official capacity. "I… It was just something I was compelled to do," she finally answered. She certainly wasn't going to get into the real reason. He didn't need to know about her parents' restaurant.

Omar nodded. "In the future, I think you should leave the detective work to the professionals. You could get yourself hurt doing what you did."

"I assure you, I'll be fine." She paused. And when she met his gaze, she had to look away. He had this way of looking at her, as though he were seeing deep into her soul.

"Mr. Ewing—"

"Omar."

"Omar," she said. "I do have to get going."

"You didn't answer me about dinner," he said.

She opened her car door. She got the sense that if she didn't get behind the wheel, he would keep talking to her. "One minute you thought I was the arsonist. Now you're asking me out on a date?"

"I wasn't asking you on a date," Omar said. "But, hey. We can always kill two birds with one stone," he added, smiling with humor.

He was unbelievable. Gabrielle knew his type. Men who thought that because they were sexy, they could have any woman they wanted. Add to that the fact that many women lost their heads over men in uniform, and she could only imagine that his ego was even more inflated.

"If you're really serious about discussing the arsonist," she began as she got into the car, "call my assistant."

She heard his soft chuckle. "Wow, you're tough. I can see why you were out on the street going after the arsonist."

"Good day, Mr. Ewing."

As she closed her car door, she heard him say, "Omar. Call me Omar."

She backed her car out of her parking space, and started to drive away. Just when she was about to turn onto the main street, she looked in the rearview mirror.

She saw Omar standing there, his arms on his hips and looking like a *GQ* model, watching her drive away.

She quickly turned right and slipped into traffic.

What the heck had just happened? Was it possible that Omar was losing his touch?

As he watched Gabrielle's Mercedes turn onto the street, he couldn't have been more surprised. He had gone to see Gabrielle to apologize, and to make amends. And she had reacted as if...

Well, she had reacted as if he had the plague.

He'd been nice, respectful. And she had treated him with disdain that he couldn't comprehend. Was there something written on his forehead that said he was a jerk?

Despite her reaction to him, there was still something about her. Something about her that got his blood pumping.

It was proving to be a challenge even to get a moment of her time.

But Omar was nothing if not up for a challenge.

Chapter 4

Gabrielle drove as if the devil were chasing behind her. Why on earth had Omar Ewing come to see her?

Her stomach was tight. Her heart was pounding. And it was aggravating.

Good Lord, Omar was sexy. While looking at him, a part of her came alive. She didn't understand this intense and idiotic attraction to a man like him.

"Forget him," she told herself.

She turned up the music as she continued driving to her parents' place. They still lived in the childhood home she had grown up in. It was a house overlooking the water, close to the beach. Her parents—Joe and Gina Leonard—had both worked two jobs when she'd been young, building the American dream for their children. Her mother used to work in a daycare during the day, while her father did construction. At night and on weekends, they cleaned office buildings. Their hard work had paid off.

Gabrielle had been ten when her parents had bought the house that ultimately became their home. It had been small, a split-level ranch house, with a huge backyard. The plan had always been to renovate the house and make it their own, something her father could do well because he worked in construction. The first order of business was to expand the house into the backyard. Her father had built his wife a dream kitchen. After that, the bedrooms had gotten bigger. An additional den had been added. Her parents had been able to renovate the house exactly to their liking. Because it had needed work and a lot of TLC, they had been able to purchase a house in a prime real estate location for an incredible price. But they had turned the house into something spectacular.

Gabrielle still remembered the celebration when the house had been finished. Her parents had been so proud. She and her sister, Grace, had been elated. And finally, her parents had stopped working quite as hard, allowing them to all spend more time together as a family.

Everything her parents had done had been for Gabrielle and Grace. She knew that. Joe and Gina had come from far more humble beginnings, and wanted their own children to have more.

Her parents had successfully conquered two goals. Raising two children, and having a house you could call a home. Now they wanted to spend their later years building another dream.

Just last year, her parents had decided to finally invest in something for themselves. For years, they had dreamed of opening a restaurant. Given that they had worked so hard to build a home for their children, her mother had not been able to follow her culinary passion when she'd been younger. Finally feeling financially secure, later in life, her parents took out some of the equity they had built up in their home to invest in opening a restaurant.

Gina's Steakhouse.

Gabrielle smiled sadly as she remembered the day the doors had opened. Her mother had beamed with such pride. Her father had insisted that the restaurant be named after his wife. After all, she had given up going to culinary school to raise a family and work to make sure food stayed on the table. Her father had wanted to make sure that her mother finally fulfilled her lifelong dream. And seeing her name on the side of a building had brought her mother incredible joy.

As Gabrielle drove, tears misted her eyes. She had been moved to tears by her mother's emotion on the day of the grand opening. Gabrielle knew that her whole life her mother had worked extra hard to make sure that she and Grace would have everything they needed in life. Finally, she had had something for herself.

But only six months after opening, the restaurant had gone up in flames.

Torched by the arsonist.

And two weeks after that, her father had his near fatal heart attack.

Gabrielle pulled into the driveway of her parents' home. She looked at the house where she had spent her happiest years. And wiped the tears from her eyes.

As she made her way to the door, she looked at the wood exterior that her father had repainted just last year. A mix of blues and yellows gave the house a cheery feel. How ironic that inside, so much sadness existed.

Gabrielle rang the doorbell. A minute later, it opened, and her mother smiled at her. "Hello, sweetheart."

"Hi, Mom," Gabrielle said. She stepped into the house and put her arms around her mother. She held her tightly, noticing that her mother seemed to shake beneath her touch.

"How's Daddy?" Gabrielle asked.

"He's hanging in there, but he's the same."

Meaning he was depressed. Gabrielle didn't know if he was more upset about the heart attack, or the restaurant burning down.

"He's upstairs?"

"Yes," her mother answered.

Ever since the heart attack, they had adjusted their master bedroom so that he could be comfortable in it and not have to move around too much. Before that, he used to love to spend time in his man cave. With her and Grace gone, her father had taken over the den. He had put a huge-screen TV in there so he could watch his favorite sports up close.

But since the heart attack, he had been spending more time in bed. Part of the reason was that he had an oxygen tank he had to use for several hours, and it was set up beside the bed. Due to his heart disease, the doctors believed his body was not getting enough oxygen, so he had been prescribed oxygen therapy.

Gabrielle had made sure that her parents had a bigger TV in the bedroom. She'd also helped her mother order a bed that could be adjusted so that her father could sit upright. Gabrielle hated to see him stay in bed all day, because to her it seemed as though he was giving up.

Gabrielle wandered through the house to the back that led up to the split-level. Her parents' bedroom was the first one on the left. Gabrielle knocked softly, then pushed the door open.

"Daddy?" she called out.

"Come in, darling."

Gabrielle stepped into the room, saw her father sitting upright in the bed. He looked exactly the same as he had the last time she had visited. A knit bedspread was thrown across his lap. His head rested on a pillow. The oxygen tubes connected to his nose.

Gabrielle's heart ached. Her father looked so darn frail. His face was worn, and his eyes were glum. Gabrielle hated this.

She walked over to her father and leaned down to give him a hug and a kiss. "Hey, Daddy."

He offered her a faint smile, but it didn't quite reach his eyes. "Hi, Gabby."

Gabrielle eased onto the bed beside her father. "How're you feeling today?"

He made a sour face. "I hate all this crap I have to eat and drink."

He gestured to the right, and Gabrielle looked on the table beside the bed. There was a tray with congealed oatmeal, a banana and a cup of nuts. "You're not eating?"

"Not that stuff." He made a face. "I made your mother get me real food."

"And what was that?" Gabrielle asked.

"Pizza." He smiled. "From that pizza place I like down the street."

"Daddy," Gabrielle said, an exasperated sigh escaping her lips. She knew exactly why her father liked that food. It was greasy and delicious—and exactly the kind of food her father had been told to stay away from. "You know you're supposed to cut out the fatty foods."

"He thinks vegetables and food cooked with less butter is torture."

At the sound of her mother's voice, Gabrielle looked over her shoulder. Her mother stepped into the room. "I've been trying to get him to follow the doctor's advice, but you see him. He's wasting away to nothing. I have to feed him."

"I know," Gabrielle said. Though she wished her mother wouldn't cave to her father's demands. Eventually, he would have to eat what was in front of him if she didn't give him an alternative.

"I need you to get better, Daddy."

"I want this arsonist caught," her father said, speaking passionately. "That's what's going to make me better. He took away my livelihood."

Her father made a pained expression and tried to adjust his body in the bed. Gabrielle's mother quickly hurried to his side. "Joe, you can't do this. You can't get yourself worked up."

"That man took away our livelihood! Our dream!"

Gabrielle took her father's hand in hers. "Daddy, you've got to take it easy. Do you want to give yourself another heart attack?"

He frowned, and huffed. But he didn't say a word.

Gabrielle squeezed her father's hand. "I'm working on finding out who did this." She looked at her mother briefly before looking at her father again. "I was close yesterday. Real close. You heard about the fire last night? Well, I was there. And I saw someone in the crowd, and—"

"You what?" her mother asked.

"I went to the scene of the fire. I wanted to look at the people, see if someone there seemed suspicious."

"Oh, my goodness," Gina uttered.

"I know I saw him," Gabrielle pressed on. "It was dark, but I tried to get a few pictures. Then, when he was leaving, I tried to follow him."

"Gabby," her father chastised. "You can't be doing that."

"There were a lot of people there. I was fine."

"I don't want you getting yourself hurt," her father scolded.

She thought of Omar, how he had echoed the same concern. Gabrielle offered her father a brave smile. "I won't get hurt. I promise you." She paused. "What matters to me is that I get this situation fixed for you."

"You always think you can fix things, don't you," Joe said. "But, Gabby, you can't. Some things you need to let the authorities handle."

"I hate seeing you like this," Gabrielle said to her father. "All the stress of what happened... I just want you to get better."

"You want me to get better, get me a chocolate fudge sundae."

"You've already had pizza today," Gabrielle said. "That's enough veering from your diet for one day."

"Joe." Gina shook her head with disdain. "You know you can't have a chocolate fudge sundae."

Joe scoffed and waved a dismissive hand. "It wasn't my diet that did this to me. It was the stress."

Gabrielle figured it was a bit of both. But mostly the stress. To lose your life's work in a flash and for no good reason was exactly why she was determined to make things right for her father. She wanted to see the light in his eyes again. And in her mother's. She couldn't walk into this house and feel this cloud of negativity hanging over all of them for much longer.

"Gabby," Gina began. "Can you come to the kitchen with me for a moment?"

Joe looked at Gina with suspicion. "What's going on?"

"I just want to talk to Gabby about dinner."

"Rib eye," Joe said as Gabrielle and her mother began to walk out of the room. "With some mac and cheese. Or maybe fries and gravy."

Gabrielle looked over her shoulder at her father. She shook her head. "Not tonight."

"Then a T-bone," Joe called as Gabrielle and her mother stepped into the hallway.

Gina turned toward her daughter. "Do you see what I have to deal with? It's so hard. I try to make him healthy meals, and he acts like I'm trying to poison him. I made him some quinoa last night, and a beautiful garden salad. He threatened to go on a hunger strike."

Gabrielle groaned. "He's acting like a petulant child. Good grief, he knows you're trying to keep him alive."

Gina linked arms with Gabrielle and walked with her toward the staircase. "Can you go to the store and pick up some groceries for me? I hate to leave him here alone. The last time I left, I came back and found him downstairs eating ice cream from the tub."

"What I can do is help you clear out the fridge," Gabrielle said. Her father wasn't an invalid. Sure, he was staying in bed a lot to rest, but he was smart enough to know that when her mother left the house, it was his opportunity to raid the fridge for the foods he really liked. "You can't have any bad stuff in the house if you don't want him to eat it."

"Later, I will clean out the fridge and cupboards of all the junk," Gina said. "In fact, I'll do it tonight."

Gabrielle doubted it. It was hard to see someone you loved beg for something and deny them. She was probably keeping the cookies and treats in the house, knowing that at some point she was going to have to placate her husband.

Her mother could no doubt use some help. Another person here to help alleviate the stress.

"Have you spoken to Grace?" Gabrielle asked.

"She says she can't get away," Gina said, answering the question Gabrielle hadn't even asked.

Gabrielle gritted her teeth. Her mother was always ready with excuses for Grace. Grace could never get away. Not unless it was something she wanted to do.

"Is she working?" Gabrielle asked.

"Not right now."

"So it would be perfect timing for her to come here and spend some time with you and Daddy," Gabrielle pointed out.

"I'm sure she's going to come here as soon as she can. She loves your father."

This wasn't about Grace not loving her father. This was about Grace being selfish. She'd been raised as a spoiled kid, and had always felt that the world revolved around her. Now her father had had a life-threatening heart attack and she didn't even have the decency to come see him? What if he had a second heart attack and died?

Gabrielle prayed that didn't happen, but there were no guarantees in life. And with her father determined to eat a diet that would kill him... You just never knew.

"It's not like we haven't heard from her," Gina said. "She's called, spoken to your father."

"Isn't that nice?" Gabrielle said sarcastically. "She should get on a plane and come down here. Portland isn't on the other side of the world."

"Don't be so hard on your sister," Gina said.

"You always defend her, Mom," Gabrielle said, exasperated. "But she's never here when we need her."

Gabrielle refrained from pointing out that her parents had always been there when Grace needed them. Grace had had one financial disaster after another in her life, and had always called her parents when she needed help picking up the pieces. While Gabrielle had adopted her parents' work ethic, her sister had not. Whenever she had money, she spent it carelessly. She liked to party, and even do the occasional recreational drug.

Though maybe it was more than occasional. That would certainly explain why she could never hold down a steady job.

"She got fired from her last job," Gina said.

"So she has no money," Gabrielle said. *Of course*, she added silently. Her sister could never keep a job. It wasn't the first time she'd been fired. And it wouldn't be the last. Grace liked to stay up late, and sleep in late. Which only proved her to be unreliable. Employers wanted to know that you would get up in the morning and go to work consistently.

But when you had Mommy and Daddy bailing you out all the time…

Gabrielle knew this wasn't the time to get into Grace's situation with her mother. So all Gabrielle said was, "Well, hopefully she finds another job and gets herself down here to see Dad."

"Will you go and pick up the groceries for me?" Gina asked.

Gabrielle put an arm around her mother. "Of course."

This was so hard on her mother, and she could see it in her eyes. If only Grace would come back home to help her parents out and ease the stress on their mother.

As Gabrielle descended the stairs with her mother, she tried to push Grace out of her mind. It hurt thinking about her sister. So many disappointments… She and her sister were not even on speaking terms anymore.

Grace had stopped talking to her because Gabrielle had refused to give her more money. The first few times Grace had called her in crisis, Gabrielle had lent her money. And when she hadn't gotten it back, she'd been okay with it. In her heart, she wanted to believe the best about her sister. Grace's hard-luck stories were always compelling. This or that bad thing had happened to her. Eventually, it became clear to Gabrielle that Grace had been making excuses.

She had a safety net. And it was the family.

So when Gabrielle had told her she would not give her any more money the last time she had called, Grace had been livid. She hadn't spoken to her since. Not truly spoken to her anyway. Gabrielle had seen her at the occasional family get-together, and Grace had always been distant and cold.

"Sweetheart?"

Her mother's voice pulled Gabrielle from her thoughts. "Yes?"

"This is a list I made. And here's some money." She stuffed several bills into Gabrielle's palm.

"I don't need the money," Gabrielle said. "I can certainly buy my parents some groceries."

"I don't know what I would do without you," Gina said and smiled.

"And I don't know what I would do without you and Daddy," Gabrielle said.

It was why she was determined to see the arsonist caught.

Because only then might some normality return to her family.

Chapter 5

"Thank you so much for coming in today," Gabrielle said to her guest, as she was packing up the clothes she had displayed on *Your Hour*. Cindy Holjak had been the last segment for today, and she had enthusiastically shown various scarves and skirts and blouses made by women in South America. All of the profit went to the women in South America, as a way to help them better their lives. It was all about empowering women in impoverished countries.

"Thank you," Cindy said. "Anytime I get to talk about this initiative, I'm grateful. This is really changing a lot of women's lives."

As Cindy continued to pack up her bags, Gabrielle retreated to the small kitchen outside the studio doors. She needed coffee.

She had stayed with her parents for a good while last night, not wanting to leave them. Her mother needed the company, she knew. Her father just wasn't the same. He was bitter, miserable. Constantly complaining about the food he had to eat. So she knew that her mother appreciated a change of pace.

Gabrielle had gotten home late, and then had not been able to sleep well. She kept thinking about her father, and how he had changed so drastically.

And all she wanted to do was be able to help him. To turn back the clock to the time before the arsonist struck.

She couldn't turn back the clock, but she could make a difference. She'd put a call in to Stacy Jackson from Channel 10 news earlier. Their team had been out videoing footage of the fire. Gabrielle was hoping that she could take a look at the footage, and see if the arsonist was anywhere in there. The first order of business when she got into her office was to check emails and her phone messages.

Her cup of coffee in hand, Gabrielle exited the small kitchen and made her way toward her office. She rounded the corner into the main reception area, then stopped dead in her tracks.

She blinked, trying to make sure that she wasn't imagining things.

"He's been waiting here for an hour," Renée the receptionist said.

Gabrielle's heart was pounding. Omar Ewing was there. Again.

"What—what are you doing here?"

"He said he wants to see you," Renée went on when Omar said nothing.

He stood up and smiled. He was wearing jeans and a white dress shirt and looked especially fine.

Gabrielle started toward the door that led to the main offices. "I thought I told you to call and set up an appointment," she said, trying to hide her irritation for Renée's benefit. "I'm certain I didn't tell you to just drop by."

"I was in the neighborhood."

Sure you were, Gabrielle thought sourly. Then she turned to Renée. "Let me know when my 2:00 appointment gets here."

Renée said, "Your 2:00?" She looked confused. "I didn't realize—"

Gabrielle shot her a narrowed gaze, and Renée caught on. "Oh. Of course. That's right, I forgot all about that appointment."

Gabrielle pushed through the door, and Omar followed her. She walked swiftly to the second door on the left, which was her office. When she stepped inside, she continued to her desk. She put her clipboard and coffee down and picked up her phone.

"What do you want, Mr. Ewing?"

"I really wish you would call me Omar."

"Whatever. Why are you here?"

"Why are you so hostile toward me?" Omar took a step toward her, and her body tensed. His large, muscular frame filled the room. She shifted uncomfortably from one foot to the other.

"I'm not being hostile."

His eyes widened. "Could have fooled me."

Gabrielle sighed softly. "It's just that I have a lot to do. And you keep showing up. It's a little annoying."

"Ouch."

Gabrielle closed her eyes and drew in a deep breath. "I'm sorry." She needed to get ahold of herself. "I'm not trying to be rude. It's just… I do have a lot of work to do."

"And one of those things is finding the arsonist," Omar stated. "Clearly, it's something you're passionate about. As a firefighter, I assure you that I'm passionate about that as well. So why don't we sit down and put our collective heads together and see what we can come up with. Maybe there's something you saw, something I saw...we both might have pieces of the puzzle that can help solve this."

It was an entirely reasonable request, and yet Gabrielle wanted to say no. But did saying no make sense? Omar had a good point. Between what he knew, and what she thought she knew, maybe they could finally nab the arsonist.

Which was what she wanted most in the world.

She just wished she could accomplish this without spending any more time with Omar.

"What are you doing tonight?" Omar asked.

Gabrielle's eyes bulged. Then she chuckled mirthlessly. "So you're asking me out to dinner again?"

"I was hoping you reconsidered."

Gabrielle picked up her coffee and took a sip. She needed this. Her temples were already throbbing, and she didn't need the added distraction of Omar Ewing.

"So, what do you say?" Omar asked. "Dinner's on me, of course."

"I have a terrible headache, and a ton of work to do—"

"Which is why you could use a break," Omar interjected. He glanced around her office. "This place is dull. Uninspiring. No wonder you have a headache. It's no place to have a meeting."

Good Lord, would he never give up?

"Pick the place, 6:00."

"Is that what works for you?" Gabrielle asked. "You give orders, and women just have to obey?"

He took another step toward her, and her heart began to race. "Consider it the doctor's orders," he said. "Because you look like you could use a prescription for fun."

"Fun! I thought you said this is about work."

"See—look how you reacted when I said the word *fun*. It's as though it's foreign to you. Yes, this is about work. But it's also about perhaps, enjoying each other's company..."

Gabrielle frowned. The problem was, she got the feeling that if she didn't say yes, Omar wouldn't go away. He was like a dog with a bone, unable to give up.

"Fine," she said.

His eyes lit up, and something about that made her stomach tickle. The idea that he *wanted* to go out with her appealed to the part of her that irrationally found him attractive.

"6:00?"

"6:00 is fine," Gabrielle said. "And you want me to choose the restaurant? Okay. There is a place on Elm Street. Italian."

"Or what about that soul food place? It's also on Elm. The play good music."

Gabrielle was about to point out that he had suggested she choose the place, but she didn't bother. "If that's what you want—"

"No, you're right," Omar said. "The Italian place will be quieter, more intimate."

Her eyes widened at the word *intimate*. "Do I have to reiterate that this is not a date?"

"It's a working date. And a place that's quieter is a better spot to talk. Especially given what we will be talking about."

"Oh. Of course."

The office phone rang, and Gabrielle could see that it was from Renée's extension. She picked up. "Gabrielle Leonard."

"It's 1:55," Renée said. "There's no one here. What do you want me to do?"

"Okay so he's been delayed by ten minutes? That's fine. There are some things I need to do before he gets here anyway," Gabrielle said into the phone, making her story up as she went along. "Thank you, Renée."

"Your appointment is delayed?" Omar asked.

"Yes, but I still have a ton of things to do before he gets here. I'm sorry, but I'm going to have to ask you to leave."

"You're not going to stand me up tonight, are you?" Omar asked.

It was tempting. Very much so. But Gabrielle knew that if she stood him up, he would just come back another day.

"No. 6:00. I'll meet you there."

Omar was smiling from ear to ear as he left the Cable Four studio building. Finally, Gabrielle was going to go on a date with him.

Well, not a date… Not according to her. But according to him, it was. She might be giving him the cold shoulder, but the heat between them was undeniable. In a setting where she could be relaxed, have a glass of wine, he was certain that her icy facade would melt.

Omar's charm had never failed him before. He didn't expect it to now.

As he reached his late-model BMW SUV, his cell phone rang. Omar dug it out of his pocket and saw Kelly Knight's face was flashing on his screen.

He made a face, wondering why she was calling him. She was a police detective, and he knew she was working the case of the arsonist. But any official business she had was with arson investigators, not him.

"Hello?" Omar said into the telephone.

"Hey, sexy."

"What's up?" Omar asked, keeping his tone businesslike. About a year ago, he and Kelly had been involved.

Their liaison had been brief and casual. Afterward, there had been no hurt feelings, and they'd remained casual friends. He and Kelly spoke only rarely these days, when work required it. Except for the occasional text, which was usually some sort of joke she was passing along.

"I was just wondering what you were doing later," Kelly said.

"Meeting a friend for dinner," Omar replied.

"Oh." Kelly sounded disappointed.

Omar's brow furrowed. She hadn't called him to get together in... Well, in a year.

"Why? Something up?"

"I was just hoping that you had some time. Maybe we could do something."

Where was this coming from? "Sorry. I don't."

"All right. I was feeling a little...frisky." She laughed airily.

"Oh." So that's why she was calling.

"When you get some time, call me," she said, her tone definitely suggestive. Then she hung up.

Omar walked the rest of the way to his car, thinking that if this had been any other time, he would have definitely taken Kelly up on her offer. Especially given that it had been a few months since he had been intimate with a woman. A dry spell for him—at least that's what the guys at the station would say. But lately, he had tired of meaningless relationships. Scratching an itch wasn't as fun anymore when he barely had two words to say to the woman in the morning.

Maybe that meant he was getting old. Maybe that meant he was getting lame.

Or maybe, it had just been that he had grown uninspired.

Until now.

No, he would not be calling Kelly at any point to take her up on her offer. The only woman he was interested in getting to know right now was the beautiful Gabrielle Leonard.

Chapter 6

Gabrielle paused as she neared Roma's, the Italian restaurant where she was meeting Omar. *Why am I doing this?* she asked herself. *Why am I going in here when I don't want to spend any time with Omar?*

So what if Omar came back to the studio again and again in a quest to get her attention? Certainly he would get the point after a while.

Swallowing, Gabrielle looked over her shoulder, at the meter where she'd parked her car. Then she looked in the direction of the restaurant once more.

While the thought that taking off and not meeting up with Omar was appealing, she also knew that it would be extremely childish. She had replayed his words to her over and over again after he'd left the studio. He hadn't said anything that could be construed as flirting, really. Perhaps the other night, but not today. He'd been courteous and businesslike. And he'd made a compelling argument for their meeting. He wanted the Ocean City arsonist caught just as much as she did.

It was that thought that had Gabrielle continuing toward the restaurant. She was doing this for her father.

She had called Stacy Jackson from Channel 10 again, but she hadn't been in the office. And again, Gabrielle had left a message. This time she had told Stacy to call her cell phone if necessary. She just wanted to hear from her as soon as possible. Stacy was her best bet at possibly being able to identify who the arsonist was. The news camera crews would have had adequate lighting, unlike her cell phone.

Gabrielle opened the restaurant door, and the smells of pasta sauce and grilled vegetables wafted into her nose. The aroma was heavenly. Her stomach grumbled, reminding her that she hadn't eaten a proper lunch. She'd only snacked on an energy bar and some coffee.

"Well, hello there."

Gabrielle was startled at the sound of his voice. Turning to look over her shoulder, she saw Omar standing in the door frame of the restaurant. And wow, he looked good. Dressed in black dress pants and a black shirt, he could easily grace the cover of magazines. He was wearing a thin gold chain around his neck, which drew her attention to the exposed area of his chest.

"Hi," she said a little breathlessly. "You were outside when I walked in?"

"I saw you just as you were stepping in. I called out to you, but you didn't hear me."

"Oh." She hadn't heard him, because she had been too absorbed in her thoughts about possibly taking off.

A young woman with her dark hair pulled back in a ponytail approached them. "Good evening," she greeted them brightly. "Table for two?"

"Yes," Omar and Gabrielle answered at the same time.

"If you could make it somewhere quiet, away from the rest of the diners," Omar said.

"A private table," the hostess echoed, her eyes dancing as her gaze flitted between Gabrielle and Omar. "Absolutely. We have a table open near the back of the restaurant that lots of couples request."

"Oh, we're not a couple," Gabrielle said. She glanced up at Omar, and saw the look of amusement on his face. Then, feeling somewhat humiliated, she turned to look at the hostess. There hadn't been any reason to tell the woman that she and Omar weren't a couple. In fact, by stating that, she was bringing more attention to the issue than was necessary. She only hoped that Omar wasn't wondering why.

The last thing she needed was for him to be thinking that she was even seeing him in that light. If only she had been smart enough to keep her mouth shut and not appear fazed at all by the hostess's assumption.

The hostess led them through the restaurant, which was half-packed. There was a table near the back of the dining room by the window that overlooked the parkette on the street. It was an area where performers came and dazzled crowds.

"A lot of people love this table, because they can look out and feel the action," the hostess said. "Yet it's private enough for a romantic... Well, it's private."

"Thank you," Gabrielle said, trying now to sound businesslike. She quickly pulled her chair back and sat. Omar made a little face, then took a seat opposite her.

"I was going to get your chair for you—"

"Not necessary. I can get my own chair."

Omar held her gaze for a moment before saying, "I'm sure you can. It's not about whether or not you are capable of pulling out your own chair. I was trying to be a gentleman."

Gabrielle drew in a deep breath. She realized that she was coming off as defensive, and there was no need for it. "I really love the fettuccine Alfredo they serve here," she said, needing to change the subject. "Have you been here before?"

"Once or twice." Omar glanced over his shoulder at the restaurant at large. "When I've been here before, it's always been packed. I can't help but wonder if people are staying away because of the arsonist."

"I certainly hope not," Gabrielle said. "It's such a shame to live our lives in fear. That's what the arsonist wants. He wants to terrorize people. I say we don't give in."

"Well, that's a moralistic argument that I can't argue with. However, people have to inject common sense into their lives."

"Are you saying I don't have any common sense?"

A beat passed, with Omar's eyes boring into hers. "Can we start over?" he asked. "Both of us take a deep breath and start again? We're not enemies."

Gabrielle closed her eyes pensively, then opened them and said, "I'm sorry. I really am. I've just been so tense these past weeks… I don't know why I'm behaving like this. I'm being childish, and I'm embarrassed."

"As long as I'm not the reason you seem so…on edge." Omar offered her a small smile.

It *was* him… At least in large part. Something about him seemed to just throw her whole body off its equilibrium. She was out of sorts, frazzled.

Aroused.

The waiter appeared then and asked if they wanted any wine. Omar looked to Gabrielle. "Your choice."

"I'd love a glass of Chardonnay."

"You want to get a half carafe?" Omar asked.

"No. I will have one glass of wine with dinner, and that's it."

Omar looked at the waiter. "Two glasses of Chardonnay, please."

"Do you like fried calamari?" Gabrielle asked. "Maybe we could share that as an appetizer?"

"I'm fine with that," Omar said.

Gabrielle took another deep breath. Omar was so much more relaxed than she was in the moment. He was going with the flow, while she was exhibiting the kind of stress one must feel when being walked to their execution. It was irrational, and unnecessary.

From here on in, she was going to present a professional and pleasant face to Omar. Because after all, weren't they here to talk about the arsonist?

Omar stood and brought his chair around to Gabrielle's side of the table. When she looked at him in surprise, he said, "You said something about getting pictures of the arsonist. It'll be easier to show them to me this way."

Gabrielle eased her chair over a little so that Omar could equally share her side of the table. "The pictures aren't great. In fact, they're really lousy because it was so dark out. All you can really see is his shape. Height, build. Sort of. I had to stay a good distance away from him so I wouldn't spook him."

"They're on your phone?" Omar asked.

Gabrielle nodded. She withdrew her phone from her purse, then swiped her screen and put in her password to unlock it. Next, she went to her gallery and opened up the photos.

She leaned in close to Omar as she showed him the first picture. "That's the guy right there. The one in the navy blue sweatshirt. Looks like it's black, I know." Gabrielle frowned. "It's totally nondescript." She swiped to the next photo. "That's the side of his face."

Omar's hand touched hers as he reached for her phone to angle it toward him. He squinted to see. "I can hardly see anything."

The waiter arrived then, and put the two glasses of wine on the table in front of them. Omar looked up at him and said, "Thanks."

Gabrielle sipped her wine before speaking. "I'm so disappointed. I wish I had better photos."

"But you got a look at him."

Gabrielle did a half shrug, half nod. "His face was somewhat boyish. By that I mean that I didn't notice any facial hair, and his skin seemed smooth. He looked to be in his early twenties."

"Is there another picture?" Omar asked.

Gabrielle swiped to the next picture. In this one, she had been able to get a shot of the man with his face turned in her direction. His head had been positioned low, as though he was deliberately trying to hide his identity. And like in the other photos, you couldn't see his face. "He knew I was watching him, I think," Gabrielle said. "Because right after I took the photo, he started to move away from me through the crowd."

"This is a better photo, but it's blurry." Omar frowned. "And you still can't see his face."

"I know. But you can see an emblem on his baseball cap. That's for the Oakland Raiders."

"An Oakland fan," Omar said. "Figures," he added, injecting a little humor. "No one who's a fan of the Ocean City Pumas could ever do this."

"I wish I'd gotten better pictures," Gabrielle said. "I feel like I've failed."

"Hey," Omar said, looking into her eyes. "You weren't out there to do a job. And it's not your job, anyway. You're a civilian. Why put it all on yourself as though you failed to discover a crucial clue?"

"I know."

The waiter returned. He recited a list of the daily specials, then asked what they wanted to order.

"Actually," Omar began, "we haven't even looked at the menu. Can you give us a few more minutes?"

"Sure," the waiter said.

"I'm really not all that hungry," Gabrielle said when the waiter had walked away. Suddenly, the idea of having an appetizer, dinner and then dessert with Omar was too much. "I'm good with an appetizer if you are."

"Maybe we can do a couple appetizers, then?" Omar suggested. He opened the menu. "You said fried calamari. How about...bruschetta, definitely. And the meatball skewers, too."

"Sounds good," Gabrielle said.

Omar lifted his glass of wine. "I'm really glad you agreed to meet me like this. Isn't it much more pleasant than being in your office?"

"The food is certainly better." Gabrielle smiled softly.

"I'm just gonna say this. And I hope you won't be mad." Omar paused. "You are incredibly beautiful."

"Why are you telling me that?" Gabrielle asked.

Omar chortled. "Well, that's not the response I expected. But do I have to have a reason to tell you that you're beautiful?"

Gabrielle shifted uncomfortably in her chair. "This isn't...it's not that kind of dinner, remember?"

"Are you really so against getting to know me?" Omar asked, his voice husky.

His head was angled toward hers, and alarm shot

through Gabrielle when she realized that he was leaning in closer. Was he going to kiss her?

She quickly jerked her head away from his. She grabbed her wine and took a liberal gulp. "So, with regard to the pictures—"

"I don't want to talk about the arsonist anymore," he said.

Gabrielle's pulse began to race. My God. He was trying to seduce her. She cleared her throat and continued, undeterred. "I'm thinking maybe I should air a description of the arsonist on my show."

Omar's expression changed instantly. Gone were the bedroom eyes, replaced with befuddlement.

"You want to publicize this on your show?" Omar asked. His tone told her that he thought the idea was crazy. "You don't even have a real description."

"I have a vague description. It might be enough for someone who knows who this guy is. The Raiders cap, general idea of the height—"

"It's a bad idea," Omar told her.

"You don't even want to hear me out?"

"I don't need to hear any more. Going public with this at this point is premature. All you will do is potentially compromise the investigation."

She laughed mirthlessly. "Compromise the investigation? This guy has been wreaking havoc on the city for months. Whatever investigations are going on are leading to nothing."

"I don't want to have this conversation again," Omar said. "You have already made it clear that you think the fire department and police are sitting on their butts doing nothing."

"You know what?" Gabrielle pushed her chair back. "I don't want to have this conversation either."

When she stood, Omar looked at her in shock. "Where are you going?"

"I'm leaving."

"Gabrielle, stay—"

She stuffed her phone into her purse. "This was a bad idea."

Gabrielle crossed paths with the waiter, whose forehead scrunched in confusion as he saw her.

"Gabrielle," Omar called.

Gabrielle headed straight for the exit, walking briskly. She didn't dare look back.

Chapter 7

Omar stared at Gabrielle's retreating form, confusion gripping him like an iron fist. In all of his years, Omar had never, ever had a woman walk out on him at a restaurant.

"Sir, is everything okay?" the waiter asked as he approached the table.

Omar quickly opened his wallet and passed the waiter more than enough bills to cover the wine. "Sorry. I've got to go."

Then he set off in pursuit of Gabrielle. He wasn't about to let her get away.

He hurried outside, saw her hustling on the sidewalk going left. He started to run. "Gabrielle!"

She quickly threw a glance over her shoulder, her eyes widening in surprise. Then she turned away from him, picking up her pace.

"Gabrielle!"

Just as she reached her car, he caught up to her. He reached out and wrapped a hand around her arm, then whirled her around.

She gasped. Did she really feel she had to run away from him? That he was going to hurt her or something? "Gabrielle, what are you doing?"

She looked down at her arm where Omar was holding her. Then she looked up into his eyes. "What are *you* doing?"

"Stopping you from leaving," he answered.

"Let me go."

She tugged on her arm, but he refused to release her. Her antic in the restaurant had been humiliating enough. "No."

Her eyes widened in disbelief as she looked at him. "I demand that you let me go."

"I give you my opinion, and you take off?"

"This whole thing about getting together... It was a mistake."

"We were in the middle of a discussion—"

"Discussion? You were telling me what to do."

"So that's why you're angry? Because I told you I don't think you should air anything about the arsonist on your show?"

"Someone in this city knows this person."

"His description could be anyone. It's not enough to broadcast."

"That's your opinion. Maybe he's spoken to someone—a girlfriend or wife or family member. Maybe someone knows a person who fits the vague description of the arsonist and this information will have them putting two and two together."

"Publicizing that picture at this point is hasty," Omar said. "Let's let the police do their work—"

"Because that has worked so well so far."

Omar looked down at her and wondered if she was always this defiant. Always so determined to have her way. "Let the police do their job. Let us do our job. We'll get this guy. We're getting closer and closer. And thanks to what you saw, we can at least narrow the suspect down to a white male."

"See? You're dismissing everything I have to say." She pulled on her arm, but he still wouldn't release it. "Omar, I want to leave."

"You agreed to dinner."

Gabrielle laughed. "I changed my mind."

Omar narrowed his eyes as he looked at her. Why was she giving him such a hard time?

"Never actually agreed to dinner. But you insisted…"

She was reading him the riot act, and he wanted her to stop. The only way that Omar could think to quiet her was to kiss her.

As the thought came into his mind, he knew it was absolutely ridiculous. This woman was not listening to reason whatsoever. And he was thinking about kissing her?

"I've always run my show with the utmost care and concern. I would not publicize the story if—"

And then he did it. He pulled her into his arms, and she gasped slightly just before his lips came down on hers. Even as he started to kiss her, he wasn't sure what he was doing. There was just so much fire between them and this was the only thing that would quench it.

Gabrielle stiffened in his arms, a moan of protest escaping her lips. But as he slipped his arms around her slim waist and pulled her against his body, he felt the moment when she surrendered to the kiss.

She softened against him, and all of the tension ebbed

out of his body. This was how he wanted her. Her lips
and body pressed against his. As she kissed him back, the
woman who seemed only able to fight with him morphed
into someone else. She was blossoming into—

Gabrielle violently pushed herself out of his arms. As
she looked up at him, her eyes shot fire. "What the heck
are you doing?" she demanded.

"Kissing you."

"I know that. But, why?"

"Seemed like the most effective way to quiet you,"
Omar muttered. And he wasn't surprised when her eyes
widened with fury.

"You are..." She shook her head, but didn't finish her
statement. He saw her eyes dart to the right, to a couple
passing by. Obviously, she wanted to contain her anger
and not draw further attention to the fact that they were
fighting.

"Sorry," Omar said. "I didn't mean that."

"Yes, you did. You invited me to dinner under false
pretenses. You acted as though you wanted to have a serious conversation about the arsonist, but you had something else in mind, didn't you?"

She was publicly scolding him on the street, and yet...
His heart was pumping wildly. What would Gabrielle be
like in the bedroom? If this fiery nature of hers extended
beyond this... He could imagine that she would be a fire-
cracker in bed.

"For one moment," he began. "For one moment, you
let down your defenses and stopped playing the angry
card. You were a woman who wanted to be kissed. To
be touched."

"That's ridiculous. And you're only saying this to me
out here in the open because you know...you know I won't
cause a scene."

"If this is what you call not causing a scene..."

She grunted in frustration. "I know exactly what your type is, Omar. I'm not flattered, nor am I interested."

"My type? Enlighten me."

"You came here with a plan. The romantic table, the wine. Dinner. Do you think I was born yesterday?"

"Amazing how you have this whole scenario figured out. That wasn't my plan, not at all."

"You really do think I'm naive, don't you? A man like you—your reputation precedes you. What happened? You ran out of other women in the city to hit on, now you're coming after me?"

"I'm attracted to you," Omar said, though God only knew why he was admitting it to her.

No, he knew why. Because something in his gut told him that all this passion—although she expressed it as anger—was actually an attempt to mask a fierce attraction. He'd felt it with that kiss. Heck, he'd felt that even before the kiss. The kiss had simply confirmed it.

"All right," he said. "I did have an ulterior motive when inviting you to dinner. That motive—to get to know you better."

She scoffed. "And how many women did you tell that last year? Heck just last week? A man like you... I won't be a notch on your bedpost."

"You are jumping to a lot of conclusions."

"Goodbye." She pressed her key remote to open her car door. Then she hustled into the driver's seat.

Unbelievable. She was taking off on him again.

Well, that's what she thought.

Omar quickly rounded the car and opened the door. She looked at him in horror as he climbed into the passenger seat beside her.

* * *

Gabrielle gasped when Omar closed her passenger side door. "What—now you're stalking me?"

"Why are you so tightly wound?" he asked without preamble.

"You lied to me. You had me come here under false pretenses. You assured me that this was just about business."

She heard Omar's deep inhale of breath as he looked into her eyes. The way he was looking at her... It unnerved her. Everything about today had unnerved her. She was completely becoming unhinged.

And then, he was touching her face. Gently. Her breath caught in her throat. She wanted to tell him to stop touching her, but she was paralyzed. His touch was electrifying.

"Are you sure that's why you're so upset?" He stroked her cheek with the pad of his thumb. "Or is it because you feel something between us. Something you don't want to admit."

Heat filled her body at his touch. She wanted to scream no, that she *wasn't* attracted to him. She didn't want him to know that he had any power over her. He was a player, like her ex-fiancé. She would be damned if she fell under his spell.

"Would it hurt you to let loose a little?" he went on.

"By let loose, you mean sleep with you."

He didn't even have the decency to deny it. Instead, he shrugged slightly. "Might help with all that tension and stress."

She pushed his hand away from her face. "Get out of my car."

"The angrier you get with me, the more I'm attracted to you. All that passion has to be coming from somewhere. There's a reason for it. And given the fact that you couldn't realistically hate me, it leads me to assume only one other thing." He stroked her hand. "That you're fighting this thing that's going on between us."

"This thing?" She forced a sarcastic laugh. "You are truly out of your mind."

"Am I? Then why is it that you can't even look in my eyes."

"I can look in your eyes." And to prove it, she met his gaze dead-on. And after only mere nanoseconds of holding his onyx gaze, she felt her skin flush.

Slowly, a smile crept across his lips. He was enjoying this! Obviously, he had pulled this sort of trick with other women. He was like a magician, knowing just how to touch a woman, just how to look at her to get the response he wanted.

Gabrielle was disgusted with herself, because she expected to be immune to those kinds of tactics. But she was proving to be mere mortal after all.

"God, I want to kiss you again."

His voice was soft. And although Gabrielle wanted to kick him out of her car, she didn't tell him to leave again. Because the idea of kissing him again...

She looked forward and gripped the steering wheel. She wasn't herself. She didn't even recognize this person that she was. A person whose body was filled with sensation and desire on a scale she hadn't experienced before.

And it was directed at the wrong man. God help her.

She faced him, saw him looking at her with those bedroom eyes of his. "I... I refuse to let you treat me like I'm some sort of plaything."

"Why do you think that's how I'm going to treat you?"

"Again, your reputation precedes you, Mr. Ewing."

"Omar."

She didn't want to call him Omar. She didn't want to

personalize anything between them. Already, she was angry with her body for its utter betrayal. She felt flushed, her womb filled with sensation.

"Why not come back to my place," Omar said, his voice husky. "End this torture for the both of us."

Her eyes grew as wide as saucers.

"God, I shouldn't have said that. It's just... Being around you... I feel... I know you feel it, too. I just want the fighting to stop."

This was torture for her, but Gabrielle doubted it was torture for him. For him, it was a game. If she went back to his place with him, she would be giving in.

He would win.

And it was that thought that finally gave her strength. Despite her throbbing body, she leveled a serious stare on him. "I've had enough of this. No means no. Please—you need to get out of my car and leave me alone."

Something flashed in Omar's eyes. A little bit of shock, maybe even hurt. Immediately she wanted to take back her words. She didn't want to make it seem as though she feared he was going to force himself on her.

But he was torturing her with all this sex talk and flirtation. And that kiss... She had wanted more.

Yet rationally, her brain knew that she couldn't get involved with a man like Omar. So she had to make the sensible decision to stay away from him.

She regretted the hurt she had caused him with her words, but she knew that if she were to take back what she'd said, she would be opening the door on this topic again. And she needed that door to remain forever shut.

Omar opened the car door and stepped outside. He leaned his head in and said, "The one thing I will never do is take advantage of a woman. Any woman I've ever been with, it's always been mutual."

He closed the door, and she quickly pressed the button to lock her car. Though she knew that at this point he wasn't going to be coming back inside. She had offended him.

But if that was the only way to guard her heart, then so be it.

Chapter 8

Sweat dripped from Omar's forehead as he pounded the punching bag in the firehouse's small gym. One. Two. Three. He punched it with all his might, grunting as he did.

Was he seriously losing his touch? Never before had he felt such heat with a woman while kissing her, only for her to turn him down so coldly.

One. Two. Three. Omar punched the bag. What was Gabrielle afraid of?

He hadn't intended to kiss her. He had only planned to simply have dinner. To give her a chance to get to know him, and find him intriguing. As other women had.

But Gabrielle Leonard was no ordinary woman. She was cut from a different cloth. A different breed.

Maybe even from a different planet, he thought, frowning.

Because of her, he had lain awake for hours in bed last night. His body had been aroused.

Because of Gabrielle.

That fire within her… How would that translate to the bedroom? Yes, he wanted to know. He couldn't deny it. That's what he had thought of as he'd lain awake at night. She was a time bomb of passion waiting to explode. And when she did, Omar wanted it to be in his arms.

God, that one kiss… He'd been filled with such an intense heat. Heat had consumed both of them. He knew that was the truth. When he felt heat with other women like that, it wasn't long before they were taking off their bras and panties and trying to get him into bed.

Yet Gabrielle had made it overwhelmingly clear that she wasn't interested.

And that whole thing about no meaning no? Omar pounded the punching bag again. He had never in his life forced himself on a woman, so for her to imply that, had really got to him.

It was the reason he had spent much of the night trying to convince himself that he had to forget her.

He assaulted the punching bag with a flurry of blows.

"Whoa, Omar."

Hearing Mason's voice, Omar turned to look over his shoulder.

"Whose face are you trying to pummel?" Mason asked.

Breathing heavily, Omar relaxed his gloved hands against the punching bag. "Just getting in a workout."

"You all right?" Mason asked. "Because you seemed distracted this morning."

"Sure," Omar said. "I'm fine."

But things weren't okay. Physically, he was fine. Emotionally…

Gabrielle Leonard had him completely out of sorts. What had happened yesterday between them had him confused and stressed out.

Women didn't treat him that way. Ever.

"You're looking pretty tense there," Mason commented.

"Just trying to stay in shape. Rescue squad... Can't afford to let my body go."

Mason chuckled. "Is that a dis, bro?"

"Naw."

"I told Sabrina I was considering the rescue squad, and she said she would kill me if I joined it. She already hates how dangerous this job is, and said she doesn't want to become a widow before she's even married."

The job did have its dangers... But that was what got Omar's blood pumping. With the greatest risk came the greatest reward.

A few weeks ago, before Christmas, a boy had fallen into a well. His frantic parents hadn't known where he was. Finally, the father had checked the property's well— and could hear the boy's faint cries.

Omar had suited up and gone down there. There were risks... Cables had been severed in the past. Sometimes, the holes were small and unable to hold two bodies comfortably. Getting stuck was a real risk.

There had been a case where a firefighter in Upstate New York had gone into such a well. There had been complications, and both he and the boy he'd been trying to save had perished. The firefighter's body had been retrieved holding the body of the boy in his arms.

At least the rescue three weeks ago had had a happy ending. Omar had been able to save the boy, and reunite him with his parents. Being able to save a life was truly rewarding.

"That's not something I have to worry about," Omar said to Mason. "I don't have a wife and kids."

"Our resident playboy will never settle down, huh?"

Omar shrugged. "Never say never."

Mason's eyes lit up. "Is there a woman in your life? Is that what this is about?"

"As if I never box in the firehouse gym," Omar commented. He wandered over to the shelf where he had put his water bottle. He shucked the gloves, lifted the bottle and took a liberal sip. Facing Mason again, he said, "So are there talks about wedding plans yet?"

"This summer," Mason said proudly. "Seriously, though. Is there a woman in your life? I saw Kelly Knight, and she said you haven't gotten back to her."

Omar made a face. "What?"

"I saw her when I went to the police station. She asked me how you were doing."

What was up with her? Omar wondered. "That's weird."

"Maybe she wants to rekindle what the two of you had last year."

"It wasn't serious," Omar said. "Just a casual fling."

"Heartbreaker," Mason joked.

"Can't please all the ladies all of the time," Omar said, adding his classical humor.

"One of these days," Mason said, "you're going to meet someone who makes you stop dead in your tracks. That woman you realize you can't live without."

"I don't know about that."

"You will. What—you want to be sixty-five and still playing around?"

"If I keep working out in the gym, I'm still gonna be this fine when I'm sixty-five."

Mason laughed. "So that's what you tell yourself at night."

Omar lifted a towel and dried his forehead. "Actually... I kind of met someone."

Mason's jaw dropped and his eyes widened. "Really? Someone you like?"

"Someone who fascinates me, yeah."

"Who is she?"

"No one you know," Omar lied. He wasn't about to tell him that he was attracted to the woman he had initially thought was the arsonist.

"Wow," Mason said. "So Omar Ewing, our resident playboy, is getting soft."

Omar looked at him, making a face. "I wouldn't call it getting soft, bro."

Mason clamped a hand down on his shoulder. "Of course not. In fact, it's amazing when you find that special person. There's nothing like it. I know I sound like a walking Hallmark card... Something I never thought possible for myself, either. But that's what love does to you."

"Well, I wouldn't go so far as to say this is love." Omar frowned. "She doesn't even want to talk to me."

Now Mason laughed. "You? There's a woman on the planet who doesn't want to talk to you? Now I know you're getting soft."

Omar smiled faintly. Firefighters were great at razzing each other. It was par for the course, and it made things interesting and fun. It also strengthened the camaraderie between them.

"The crazy thing is, she's been cold to me, but I still want to get to know her. If another woman treated me like this, I'd be gone. But this one... The more she pushes me away, the more I want to get to know her." Omar took another swig of his water. "But I can't force myself on her. She made it pretty clear she's not interested."

"So you're giving up?"

Omar shrugged. "What else can I do?"

"You can be the Omar we all know and love." Mason

smiled at him. "Omar who knows how to go after what he wants. If you really feel something for this girl, why give up without a fight? This is the first time that I ever think I've heard you talk about someone like this. Clearly you like her. And that's a great thing. She just sounds like the kind of girl you have to work hard for."

"I'm kind of afraid that if I try to see her again, she's going to have a restraining order slapped against me."

"Well, if she does, then you'll really know she's not interested. But maybe she's one of those women who is a little harder to get. Not the kinda woman that you're used to. You know… The ones who basically worship the ground you walk on."

"I don't know, man."

"Well, if you like her that much, I wouldn't give up." Mason said.

After Mason left the gym, Omar thought about what he'd said. For the first time in a long time, he had met a woman who actually made him feel sparks. The kind of sparks he hadn't felt in years. Gabrielle wasn't just a woman with a pretty face whom he could imagine having a few casual hours of fun with.

She was getting under his skin. And yet she wouldn't give him the time of day.

Omar got into the shower, still thinking about Gabrielle. She'd made a comment about his reputation preceding him. Omar knew that among the firehouses, the guys thought he had a different woman in his bed every other night. It wasn't true. But how would Gabrielle have that idea of him? He didn't know her. And he didn't know anybody who knew her. At least not that he was aware of.

By the time he was getting out of the shower, he knew

that he had to see her again. The kiss they had shared... The entire energy between them... Mason was right. How could he just walk away?

Gabrielle sat at her desk, squeezing the life out of her tension ball. She was still furious about what had happened last night with Omar.

As she had driven off, she'd wanted to scream at the top of her lungs. Just being near Omar made her feel like she was losing her mind.

He'd kissed her. He'd taken her into his arms on the street and kissed her! How dare he?

Maybe she had only herself to blame. Her instincts had told her not to go to dinner with him. She already knew he was a player. Yet she had gone, believing that he truly wanted to see her about the serious issue of the Ocean City arsonist. All he had really wanted was a chance to try and seduce her.

Gabrielle should have slapped him when he kissed her. Men like Omar... They thought all they had to do was kiss a woman and she would be dropping her panties... and thanking him afterward.

Well, he had another think coming.

Her heart had pounded furiously as she had driven home. She'd been livid. And was still angry.

But even angrier because of the truth she couldn't deny. In some odd way, she'd been aroused.

No, not aroused, she told herself. *How could I ever be aroused by a man like Omar?*

Worse, she couldn't help thinking that he had kissed her as a way to get her to obey him. He didn't want her airing the story about the arsonist. But somebody knew who he was. Somebody might see the picture—no matter how blurry—and it would click in their brain that they knew who the person was. How could she not air the photo?

She was an adult, a professional. She could make up her own mind about the right thing to do. Omar's mind had clearly not been even anywhere near where it should have been. Not with the bedroom eyes he had been giving her, and the kiss he'd had the nerve to lay on her. She was certain that the only reason he had met her for dinner was because he wanted a chance to seduce her.

No, she would make up her own mind about what to do with the photos she had taken. Gabrielle had run the idea by Janine the station manager and Janine had been excited. The idea that they might have evidence that could crack the case wide-open? For Janine, it was a no-brainer.

And if this led to the arrest of the arsonist, Gabrielle would finally have justice for her father.

Chapter 9

Omar was eating an early breakfast near the end of his twenty-four hour shift at the firehouse the next morning when a newspaper was tossed onto the table beside him. He glanced at it briefly before looking up and seeing that Tyler was the one who had put it on the table.

"Check it out," Tyler told him.

Omar looked at the headline of the paper. And as he read it, he felt fire burning in his veins.

DO YOU KNOW THIS ARSONIST?

He put his fork down at the side of his plate, the scrambled eggs and hash browns forgotten. Picking up the paper, he said, "This is today's paper?"

"Hot off the press," Tyler told him.

Omar shook his head and muttered, "I can't believe she did it."

"What was that?" Tyler asked.

Omar looked up at him. "That reporter from the cable

station. I spoke to her yesterday. Told her not to put this out there."

Tyler pulled out the chair next to Omar, and sat. Omar explained that Gabrielle had gotten some pictures of the elected arsonist, and how he had tried to reason with her to go to the police as opposed to broadcasting on air.

"No doubt, the police will have to field a lot of calls after this," Tyler said. "Hopefully, it will lead to something."

Omar looked at the three pictures that had been included on the front page. They were all far too dark and grainy. The only thing you could truly make out was the Oakland Raiders hat.

Groaning in frustration, Omar tossed the paper onto the table beside him. Was Gabrielle really so hell-bent on proving that no one could tell her what to do that she would go ahead with a move like this? For one thing, they were dealing with an arsonist. What kind of harm was she possibly putting herself in?

"The article says the story first broke on Cable Four news."

"Of course it did," Omar said sourly. He wondered if he could access the video online. Standing, he pulled his cell phone out of his pocket. Within a minute, he had the cable station's website loaded up. And right there, one of the thumbnails held the same caption. DO YOU KNOW THIS ARSONIST?

Walking out of the mess hall, Omar pressed for the video to play. Gabrielle's beautiful face came into view after the mandatory advertising.

"Good morning, Ocean City," she said. "Thank you for being with me today. As you know—as we all know—an arsonist has gripped our city with fear. Just last month, firefighter Dean Dunbar was laid to rest after a fire started by the arsonist took his life." A photo of Dean, in his firefighter uniform, appeared on the bottom right of the screen. "I don't know about you, but I'm tired of this. Enough is enough."

She was staring into the camera, making it seem as though she were speaking to every person, personally. "This man was spotted at the scene." She held up two photos. One that showed the Oakland Raiders hat, and the other that showed the side profile of the man's face. "Now, I know these pictures aren't very clear. But I also know that somebody out there knows who this is. He's a white male, around 5 foot 11. Dark hair. As you see, his face is obscured with the cap he is wearing. But what you can also see is that the hat has the emblem for the Oakland Raiders. So this person is likely a Raiders fan." She paused briefly. "This picture might strike a memory in you. You might recognize this side profile. And if you do, I am begging you to contact the police. Or if you don't want to call the police, contact our station. We will help you. It's time we end this reign of terror in our city. We deserve to be able to walk around and go to restaurants without worrying if that may be the last thing we do."

Omar shook his head, not believing what he had just seen. The guy was wearing an Oakland Raiders hat, but it could have been part of the disguise. Maybe he wasn't a Raiders fan.

Why hadn't Gabrielle gone to the police with this information?

And worse, had she just gotten the arsonist's attention?

When the knock sounded on her office door, Gabrielle looked up. The door inched open, and Renée peered in.

"Yes, Renée?"

"Um, that firefighter is here to see you again?"

After he had dropped by the other day, Gabrielle had explained to Renée that he was a local firefighter. She had told a white lie about him wanting to be on her show. Now, she hoped Renée wouldn't realize that she hadn't been truthful with her.

"Tell him I'm busy."

Suddenly, he appeared in her doorway. Gabrielle's eyes widened, and her stomach lurched. He was wearing a T-shirt that had the emblem of the Ocean City Fire Department on it, and a pair of denim jeans. Casual clothes, yet he looked anything but casual.

He looked amazing.

Clearly, Renée thought so as well. Because she couldn't take her eyes off him.

"I'm sure you can spare a moment or two for me," he said. He held up a folded newspaper, and she knew that he had seen her story.

And knew that he was upset by it.

"Fine," Gabrielle said. "I've got a few minutes."

Renée slipped out of the office, and behind Omar's back, she caught Gabrielle's gaze and feigned fanning herself because of his hotness. Then Omar shut the door.

He had a determined, if not downright unhappy, look on his face. Gabrielle stood from behind her desk and smoothed her hands over her blazer. She braced herself—because she knew he was about to give her a piece of his mind.

"Do you have a death wish?" Omar asked her.

Gabrielle tried to appear unfazed. "Mr. Ewing, I have work to do."

"Yeah, that's obvious," he quipped. "I saw your show. You shared the photos of the arsonist."

She crossed her arms over her chest. "Yes, I did."

"Did you attend the police academy in your spare

time?" he asked. "Because you seem to think you can handle taking down a criminal on your own."

Gabrielle's jaw tightened. "I run a TV show. I don't need your permission or anyone else's—"

"You're being reckless," Omar interjected. "If this person is crazy—and clearly he is—then what you're doing is goading him."

"Or, I'm making it impossible for him to hide." She sighed. Why didn't he get her point? "Somebody in this town knows who he is."

"I told you not to air those photos. I told you to go to the police and let them handle this. I don't understand—"

"You don't understand why I didn't listen to you after you kissed me?" She scoffed. "Do you really think I'm some naive woman who's going to be affected by your charms?"

A look of confusion came over his face. "That's not why I kissed you."

"Oh, it isn't?"

"I kissed you because—and God only knows why— I'm attracted to you. But I'm not used to women hearing reason and deciding to act on emotion."

"So now you're belittling me?" She didn't want to fight again. She was still tense from their clash outside the restaurant.

Omar stepped toward her, and she flinched as he neared her. Not because she was afraid, but because everything about him had her nerves frayed.

"Did you stop to think about what the consequences of your actions could be? If the arsonist thinks that your pictures of him will actually help bring him down, how do you know he won't lash out at you?"

"I refuse to be terrorized by this—this monster. Whoever he is. And I believe that the citizens of Ocean City—"

"I don't want to hear your high horse spiel." He groaned in frustration. "I would have expected a little bit of professional courtesy from you. Instead, it seems as though I should've told you *to* do it—then you wouldn't have."

"So you think my decision was based solely on what you thought I should do?"

"Are you gonna tell me you didn't do it in spite even in the least?"

"I don't make my decisions based on you," she told him, and raised her chin in defiance.

"I don't believe that. You were angry at me for kissing you. And you did this specifically because I told you that you shouldn't."

Gabrielle said nothing.

He took another step closer, and her heart slammed against her rib cage. Good Lord, was he going to kiss her again?

Her breathing quickened. What was wrong with her? She didn't want him to kiss her. She didn't want to feel his arms wrapped around her. She *didn't...*

"Maybe you think this is some kind of game. Or maybe this is about advancing your career. I don't know. But what you just did... I'm worried about you."

"I can take care of myself."

He shook his head as he looked at her. "I don't think I've ever met anyone like you."

"I'm sure you haven't. I take that as a compliment."

"You're so defiant that you can't get it through your head that what you did was dangerous? Or do you think this is a game? Because if this is about a quest on your part to build your résumé so you can go to a bigger city and get a cushier job..."

"This isn't about me getting a better job. It's not about the notoriety at all."

"Then what is it about?" he asked her.

Gabrielle felt a myriad of emotions at his question. She turned away from him momentarily, needing to compose herself. Then, drawing in a deep breath, she faced him again. "It's about catching the person who destroyed my family's life." When his eyes narrowed with confusion, she added, "My parents were his victims. He burned down their restaurant."

Chapter 10

Omar's lips parted, but he didn't know what to say. He certainly hadn't expected Gabrielle to say that.

He stared at her, at her arms folded over her chest. At the way her bottom lip trembled slightly.

Finally, he understood.

"Why didn't you tell me this sooner?" he asked.

Gabrielle shrugged. "I don't know."

"Which restaurant?"

"Gina's Steakhouse. It had only been open for six months before the arsonist torched it. It was their dream. My mother always wished she could have gone to culinary school, but she never got the chance. That didn't stop her from cooking at home. She made delicious dishes. But she always had this dream of owning a restaurant. Finally, after my parents worked so hard for their entire lives to provide for me and my sister, they were investing in themselves. They were so happy…until the arsonist struck."

"I'm sorry," Omar said softly.

"And now, everything has changed."

"I can't presume to tell you I know how hard this is, but they can rebuild, right? They had insurance?"

Gabrielle laughed sarcastically. "Rebuild? Two weeks after the fire, my father had a heart attack. He nearly died. Right now, his health is still touch and go. The stress of everything that happened almost cost him his life." She brushed at her eye. "So, no. They can't just rebuild."

Omar didn't know what to say. All he knew was that as he looked at her, he wished he could offer her comfort. "I didn't know."

"How could you know? You think I'm reckless but I'm determined. Determined to take down this man who nearly killed my father."

Omar stepped toward her and gently put a hand on her face. "I get it. I do. But you can't do this alone. You don't know who you're dealing with. And God knows I hate to see you put yourself in harm's way."

"He's a coward. I'm not afraid of him."

Omar had seen this kind of irresponsibly brave stance before. With Mika, fifteen years ago. Mika had believed she shouldn't have to live her life in fear. She was determined to live her life as she saw fit. Determined not to let fear hold her back.

Now she was in a grave.

Instead of telling Gabrielle what she should do, Omar tried a different tactic to get through to her. "I don't want to see anything happen to you."

"Why? I'm not your problem."

Not his problem? Did she really think that he wouldn't care if she got hurt?

He wanted to shake some sense into her. He wanted to kiss her. But most of all, he wanted to keep her safe.

"Now you know the situation," she said. "I can't stop until this arsonist is caught."

If she was determined to put herself in harm's way, then he was going to have to look out for her. "What time do you leave work today?"

"Why?"

"Please, just answer the question."

A beat passed. "I usually leave around 5:30."

"Good. I'll be back."

"What?"

He turned to look over his shoulder at her when he was about to open the office door. "I'll be back. If the arsonist saw your story, who knows what he might be thinking right now. He might want to lash out at you."

"I highly doubt that."

"Doesn't matter. I'm gonna come back here at 5:30 this evening to make sure you get home okay."

"That's completely unnecessary," she said. Gone was the vulnerable Gabrielle, replaced with the strong-willed woman he had come to know.

"It's not a question," he told her.

Then he opened the door and left her office.

Gabrielle couldn't help but chuckle when Omar left. Oh, he was smooth. No doubt about it. At least he thought he was.

Make sure you get home okay... Did he really think she was that naive?

She'd seen a gentler side to him today, one she hadn't expected. But just because he was a player didn't mean he lacked compassion. He felt for her, for her parents. And that was nice. But she wasn't about to let him follow her home because he feared the arsonist might be following her.

It was a ploy. And perhaps this was the next step in the player's handbook. She had been refuting his advances so far. Now, maybe he wanted her to feel vulnerable and afraid. Then he'd come in as the hero who would rescue her.

"Of course," she muttered. "You think you're so smart, Omar."

But she was going to outwit him at his own game.

She picked up her cell phone and punched in her best friend Pauline's number. Pauline answered after two rings.

"Hey, Gabby," Pauline said brightly. "I was just thinking about you."

"You were? Are you thinking margaritas and Mexican food?"

"You read my mind," Pauline said.

"6:00? Our favorite place?"

"I'll see you there."

Gabrielle ended the call and smiled. When Omar came back, he wouldn't be able to follow her home. Because she would be going out to meet her friend.

Obviously, Omar's true goal was to find out where she lived. Once he had her address, perhaps he would pay her an unexpected visit. See if he could break down her defenses and seduce her at her own door.

She did understand Omar's apprehension, and she would certainly be cautious going home. But that caution included not letting her guard down where Omar was concerned.

She could only imagine that women didn't reject him, which was probably the reason he seemed even more intent on spending time with her. He probably couldn't understand why he hadn't had her swooning already.

And yet, she *had* swooned a little. Even now when

he had come to see her again, she'd felt an odd flush of warmth. Felt it, and hated it.

She wasn't attracted to him. Of course she wasn't. But she was, perhaps on some level, irrationally flattered. She was a woman, and he was an attractive man. The very fact that he was showing any interest—and in such a dogged way—that had to be why she felt any flush of anything where he was concerned.

Gabrielle needed to see Pauline. Gabrielle had spent so much time thinking about the arsonist and trying to figure out who he was that the stress was getting to her. And nearly losing her father… She needed a break.

And she knew that she could trust Pauline to help her put things in perspective where Omar was concerned.

At 5:25 p.m., Renée came to Gabrielle's office door. "Omar the firefighter is back," she said in a singsong voice.

Omar the firefighter… Good grief, was Renée enamored with the fact that he was a firefighter? Was she—like other women—intrigued by a man in uniform?

"Thank you, Renée. Tell him I will be right out."

Minutes later, Gabrielle was heading into the main entrance area of the station. Omar, who had been sitting, stood to meet her. "Hello, Gabrielle."

"Hi." She continued walking, heading to the exit door.

He followed her outside to the parking lot. Once at her car, Omar quickly stepped in front of her, and began to examine her vehicle. He even got onto his knees and looked beneath it.

"Is this really necessary?" Gabrielle asked.

Omar didn't answer, just hopped back up to a standing position and brushed his hands together to get off the debris from the asphalt. "Looks clear. Now, I was able to park my car at the back of the building. If you just wait here, I will pull out so I can follow you home."

Gabrielle had to fight to hide her smirk. "Actually, that's not going to happen."

"I already told you, it's not up for debate."

"First of all, I'm not listed," Gabrielle said matter-of-factly. "So even if the arsonist is upset with me and looks up my name in the phone book or online, he won't be able to find out where I live."

"I would still feel better if—"

"I have plans," Gabrielle said simply.

Omar narrowed his eyes as he looked at her. "You didn't mention that before."

"It just came up," she told him. "And I didn't have a way to reach you..."

Gabrielle could see the suspicion written all over Omar's face. "We had a plan," he told her.

"Yeah, well... The plan changed. My best friend called, she... Needs to see me. I couldn't very well tell her no." It was a little white lie. But Omar didn't need to know any different.

Gabrielle heard his groan of frustration. "Gabrielle..."

"Omar, you're worrying yourself needlessly. I'm going to be fine." She walked around to the driver side door, then pressed her remote to open it. "I'm meeting my friend for dinner." When he continued to look at her with disappointment, she said, "Why don't you give me your number? If I see anything suspicious, I promise I will call you."

He took a step toward her. "You're running away," he said softly.

She looked up at him, into deep eyes that were filled with heat, and she felt her womb tighten with lust. She quickly averted her gaze.

"See, you can't deny it," he said.

Suddenly, Omar was touching her. His fingertips delicately skimmed up her arm. Pleasure shot through her body at the simple touch. And for a moment, she wanted to lose herself in his touch. She wanted to escape all of the unpleasantness of the recent weeks and just let go.

She wanted him to kiss her again. She wanted to feel his mouth on hers, because that one taste of him had been so sweet...

As heat flooded her body, she was angry with herself. *What was she thinking?* She didn't want Omar to kiss and touch her—not at all.

She hated how he distracted her with his touch. It must have been some sort of skill. But her senses quickly returning to her, she said, "I'm not running. I'm going out to dinner with a friend."

Then she took a step backward, breaking the physical contact between them. She couldn't have him touching her and be able to think clearly.

But something about the look in his eyes gave her pause. Was he really worried about her? She had assumed that his suggestion that he follow her home was simply a ploy to figure out where she lived. But she saw genuine concern in his expression.

"Seriously," she said. "I'm going to be fine. But, like I said, I can take your number."

She could see in his eyes that he wasn't going to argue with her any further. And she was grateful for that. "Anything suspicious," he said. "Anything at all."

Gabrielle took her phone from her purse. "Let me put your number into my phone. What is it?"

Omar recited his phone number, and Gabrielle read it back to him. "Why don't you text me, make sure it goes through."

Again, Gabrielle had to fight a smirk. She wanted his number—without having to give him hers. "I got it," she said.

Then she opened her car door and got in. Finally, she allowed herself to smile.

She had just outwitted the player at his own game.

Chapter 11

When Gabrielle saw her friend being led to their table in Casa Prickly Pear, she got to her feet and smiled. Just seeing Pauline had already put her in a better mood. Some of the tension in her shoulders and neck began to ebb away. Pauline would help focus her back on the task at hand, give her ways to put Omar out of her mind.

Pauline was that kind of girl. Though she'd married the man she believed was the love of her life, when she realized they were on two different paths, she didn't waste time. Yes, she tried to see if things could be salvaged. But when she knew they couldn't, she moved on.

Pauline hurried across the restaurant floor toward her, beaming. Her natural hair was styled in an afro, and she was wearing a hot pink headband that matched her hot pink shirt. Her tight jeans highlighted her shapely figure. As usual. She had curves, and liked flaunting them.

"Hey, Gabrielle," she said as she reached the table. "Sorry I'm late."

"No worries," Gabrielle said. "I've only been here about ten minutes."

Pauline slipped into the other side of the booth. "Traffic was bad. There's an accident on Chippewa Street. Firefighters are out there and everything."

Firefighters... The very mention made Gabrielle's stomach tighten. Would she not be able to hear the word *firefighters* without thinking of Omar?

Of course she would.

"Sorry," Gabrielle said, and gestured to the complimentary bowl of tortilla chips and salsa. "I already ate most of the chips."

"Did you eat today?" Pauline asked.

"I had an energy bar. And a few coffees."

"It's a new year, and you have got to change your diet. You can't live on espressos and energy bars. It makes you too high-strung. Not to mention it's completely unhealthy."

"I plan to eat well tonight." And to emphasize that point, Gabrielle scooped up another chip. "These are so good."

"So, what's up?" Pauline asked. "You seemed a little stressed out when you spoke to me earlier."

"I did?"

"Yeah."

Pauline had been her best friend since second grade, so it made sense that she was able to read Gabrielle's mood. Other people had come and gone in her life, but Pauline had been a constant. Six years ago, Gabrielle had been the maid of honor at Pauline's wedding. Just two years after that, Gabrielle had thrown Pauline a divorce party. They were BFFs and always would be.

Pauline lifted a chip from the bowl on the table, and

as she munched on it, she glanced around the restaurant. "Any available guys here?"

"I didn't look."

Pauline twisted her lips as she faced Gabrielle. "Wasn't that on your New Year's resolution list? To start dating in the New Year?"

"That was on *your* New Year's list for me, and I don't think that counts." Somehow, despite Pauline's failed marriage and other disappointments in her life, she had managed to stay positive and upbeat. It was one of the reasons that Gabrielle loved her so much. When they were kids, Pauline could talk Gabrielle out of any funk. And she could still do the same today.

"You said you would start dating again," Pauline said.

"So you just expect me to walk into a random place and pick someone out?"

"You know what they say. The best way to get over someone is to get under someone else." Pauline wiggled her eyebrows.

For a moment, Gabrielle thought about getting under Omar. She knew that he would be able to please her in the bedroom. Everything about him screamed that he was an amazing lover.

She quickly grabbed a chip and munched on it. "What about you? Are you going to get under someone new?"

"Me?" Pauline asked. "Gary and I just broke up before Christmas. The relationship wasn't that serious, but still, I'm taking a little time."

"Ah, so what's good for the goose isn't good for the gander?" Gabrielle asked, looking at her friend with a pointed expression.

"You and Tobias broke up what—seven or eight months ago? And it's not like Gary dumped me. I dumped him, so I've already had my closure."

True to Pauline's nature, when she had realized that her relationship with Gary was going nowhere, she had ended it swiftly. And she'd made sure to do so before the holidays, because she felt it was cruel to lead him on over the holidays when she knew there was no future.

Pauline finished munching on another chip. "So our situations are totally different," she continued. "Besides, I'm not sulking."

Gabrielle's jaw dropped, then she frowned. "I'm not sulking." *Was* she sulking? "Well, maybe I am. You know what I'm going through."

"I do," Pauline said, her tone getting serious. "How's your dad doing?"

"He's hanging in there. Fussing that he can't eat all the *real* food he used to eat. He's giving my mother a hard time." Gabrielle picked up a chip and dipped it into the salsa bowl. "It's as if he's incapable of understanding that the changes the doctors are telling him to make are to save his life."

"He must," Pauline said. "He just doesn't like it. In time, he'll get used to it."

"My mother is stressed out, and I know she's caving to his demands. At least at times. And my sister… Of course she's MIA."

Tara, the young woman who was their regular waitress, came over to the table with a big grin. "Hey, Pauline. You made it."

"You know I never miss a chance to eat here," Pauline responded.

"Are you two going to be adventurous tonight?" Tara asked. "Or are you going to go with the chicken fajitas?"

Gabrielle smiled slyly. "You know us so well."

"And two frozen lime margaritas with salted rims?" Tara asked.

"You know it," Pauline said. "And when you get a chance, can you bring out another bowl of chips?"

The restaurant offered as much free chips and salsa as you could eat. It was one of the perks of coming there. The downside, a person was often full by the time the meal came around.

"Sure thing," Tara told them.

As she walked away, Pauline reached for a chip and scooped out some salsa sauce to go along with it. "So, what else is going on?"

"What do you mean?" Gabrielle asked.

Pauline made a face as she looked at her. "I can sense it. Something else is going on."

Gabrielle sighed.

"After over twenty-five years of being friends, I can read you like a book. And I think something else is bothering you besides your father. Granted, I know that's tough to deal with. But he's strong. He'll be okay."

Gabrielle nodded. "I have to believe that." Pauline had helped her get through that horrifying day when her father had had his heart attack. "But he's still so angry. He put so much into that restaurant, only to have it burned down. I worried that the added stress will do him in."

"Everyone at my office was buzzing about the newspaper article and your show," Pauline said. "Any leads?"

"Not that I know of. I heard from a police officer, he wanted to interview me. So I did that this morning. Stacy Jackson from Channel 10 also got back to me. But their cameras were never focused on the crowd, only the fire. So that was a dead end."

"It's only a matter of time," Pauline said. "I truly believe that." She looked Gabrielle in the eye. "Is that it? Everything that's bothering you?"

"Well, Dr. Pauline…" Gabrielle offered her a small

smile. Then she decided to bring up the issue at hand. The real reason she had needed to meet with her friend tonight. "Remember how I told you about that firefighter who thought I was the arsonist that night at the fire?"

"How could I forget? That was crazy."

"I can't seem to shake him."

Pauline looked at her with a confused expression. "What does that mean?"

"He keeps coming around. He insisted that we get together to discuss what I knew about the arsonist. Now, because I went on air with the description, he showed up at the station again today. He was practically fuming because I shared those photos of the arsonist. He talked about how I was putting myself in harm's way."

"So he's worried about you."

"It was an excuse to see me."

"So he's interested in you," Pauline supplied.

Gabrielle made a face. Pauline would see the positive in anything she said. "He showed up because he was hoping to follow me home to make sure I was safe." Gabrielle made air quotes around *to make sure I was safe* and rolled her eyes. "As if I were born yesterday."

Pauline's eyes lit up. *"And you're here with me?"*

"Don't say that. I'm completely uninterested in him. Honestly, I think he just wants to sleep with me. He insisted that I meet him at a restaurant so we could talk about the case. Then he made sure we had a private table. I think he was hoping that if he gave me a good meal, I would be so impressed that I would drop my panties."

"That wouldn't be such a bad idea," Pauline said, giving her pointed look.

Gabrielle gaped at her friend. "You did not just say that."

"Would it be so bad?" Pauline asked. "I think it would

do you a world of good if you were to lighten up a little and get your groove on."

"Pauline!" Gabrielle said. She was about to say more, but Tara appeared, so she bit her tongue and smiled, gracefully accepting the drinks and waiting until Tara was out of earshot before she continued. "How could you say that?"

"Because. First of all, we were just talking about how the best way to get over someone is to get under someone else."

"*You* were talking about that."

Pauline picked up a fresh, warm tortilla chip. "And you really need to get over Tobias once and for all."

"What are you talking about? I'm over Tobias."

"Really?" Pauline asked, her tone sarcastic.

"If you think I'm sitting around wishing that he were back in my life, then you don't know me as well as you think you do."

"I'm not saying that," Pauline said. "But you *have* been in this funk ever since he left."

"Tobias didn't leave. I kicked him to the curb."

Pauline didn't look convinced, but didn't exactly disagree. "You set him up for failure. And once he failed, you dumped him."

"You blame me for dumping him after he slept with my cousin?" Gabrielle asked, sounding incredulous.

"No," Pauline said. "Of course not. But that's my point. It's over, you know it, and you're not pining over him or anything. Yet you're just not yourself. It's like there's a dark cloud hanging over you."

"My parents' restaurant was burned down," Gabrielle said, stating the obvious. Such a traumatic event was enough to have anyone distracted. "Of course I'm stressed and preoccupied."

Pauline started shaking her head even before Gabrielle finished speaking. "The dark cloud happened before that. Ever since Tobias moved to Phoenix with your cousin…"

Gabrielle took a sip of her drink. She didn't need nor want to be reminded of Tobias's betrayal. "Why are we talking about my ex?"

"Because," Pauline began, then scooped up another tortilla chip. "We were talking about the fact that you could use a little hot action in your life to get over your past."

"We were not talking about that."

"Yeah, well we should have been," Pauline said. "It's a new year, and you need to meet someone. Now you tell me you have, and he's into you? And you don't want to jump on that?"

"You have lost your mind," Gabrielle commented. "My issue… The tension in my life… It's not coming from lack of sex. It's coming from what happened to my father, and the fact that I need to find this person who burned my family's restaurant down. Because that's probably the only thing that's going to help my father feel better, which will help him avoid another heart attack. You're not listening to anything I'm saying."

"I'm sorry," Pauline said. "All I'm wondering is if this firefighter is hot?"

"Is that the only thing that matters?"

"It matters. For what you need, it matters." Pauline paused. "I'm not saying look for a love connection, okay? I'm just saying find a hot bod that will help you escape. I can see the tension in your shoulders. You need to unwind, girl."

"I don't need a guy with a one-track mind, Pauline."

"That's exactly what you need!"

Gabrielle glanced nervously around the restaurant.

"Can you please keep it down? Everyone doesn't need to know we're talking about my sex life here."

"What sex life?"

Gabrielle sighed in exasperation. "You're too much."

"I'm speaking the truth," Pauline said. "And worse, it's like you have a brick wall erected around you like armor to keep every guy out."

Did she? "Pauline, this guy is a player. A friend of a friend dated him a couple years back. Turned out he was involved with two other women, so there was this crazy love triangle. Both of the women ended up devastated. So sure, he's probably a great lover. I don't doubt he has enough experience. But I'm not a one-night stand kind of girl. And even if I were to consider that, it would have to be with a guy that I felt was worthy of me."

Worthy of her... Who was she kidding? A part of her knew that if she were to scratch her seven-month itch, Omar would be a perfect guy to fit the bill. The chemistry building between them was off the charts—and she knew it.

She just didn't like it.

"You are wound up tighter than a corkscrew, my friend," Pauline said to her. "You are completely overthinking things. All you need is someone who is willing, and able. This other stuff you are talking about... It's like white noise."

Gabrielle sipped her drink. For Pauline, it was either black or it was white. She didn't sweat the small stuff. Which, obviously, contributed to her happy-go-lucky nature. Nothing ever seemed to truly get her down, or steer her off course. Not even the downfall of her marriage. Yes, she grieved over the loss of her marriage like any normal person. But she had bounced back easily.

"So I shouldn't even consider his character?"

"The way I see it, you just need to consider the chemistry between the two of you. If you feel something, go for it."

"I'm not sure why you of all people are saying this. It's not like you would run around doing something like that. You took your time getting back into the dating scene after your marriage. It was at least what—a year and a few months before you started dating anyone else?"

"Dating seriously, yeah." Pauline said. "I'm not saying you're looking for your next fiancé. Good grief. I'm just saying to have some fun."

"With a man like that?"

"That kind of guy is perfect," Pauline said. "You don't have to worry that there's a serious commitment going on. You don't have to wonder if he's stepping out on you. Because you don't care. You use protection, and you enjoy yourself." She took a sip of her margarita. "How do you think I dealt with Steve and I breaking up?"

Gabrielle narrowed her eyes as she looked at her friend. "You certainly never told me that you started sleeping around…"

"I didn't *sleep around*. But—there was this guy at the gym—sexy and he knew it. And he knew that I knew it. He also knew that I wasn't looking for anything serious. One thing led to another and we got involved for a bit."

Gabrielle stared at Pauline in disbelief. "You never told me that."

"Because I didn't want you to judge me. And what can I say? It was what I needed at the time. Yes, I'm hoping that I'll find that guy who sweeps me off my feet. But what I really needed once it was over with Steve was to get out of my funk. Every woman needs a guy to rock her world once in a while. Know what I'm saying?" She popped another chip into her mouth.

"I can't believe you're saying this to me."

Tara appeared with the fajitas and placed the sizzling pan onto the table. When she was gone, Pauline continued. "I don't believe you're any different than any other girl out there. We all need a palate cleanser before we can move forward with our lives."

"Wow," was all Gabrielle could say.

"And you just described the perfect guy to cleanse your palate with. If I were you, I would stop complaining and take it as a blessing."

Chapter 12

Later, when Gabrielle was home alone after her dinner with Pauline, she found herself looking online for pictures of Omar. She didn't find him on any social network site. *Maybe he's involved with too many women to put himself out there publicly*, she thought, scoffing.

What she did find were articles about his heroism. He was a part of the Ocean City Fire Department's rescue squad, which meant he performed a lot of high-risk rescues. Most recently, he had saved a child who had fallen into a well. He had pulled families from burning buildings, saved a woman who was drowning in her car...

He'd even received commendations from the city.

On paper, he was certainly a stand-up guy.

She clicked another link where she saw his name highlighted. And a page with three partially dressed firefighters popped up on her screen.

"Oh, hello," she said, despite herself. The pictures of the men were gorgeous. Especially the one of Omar...

It was an article about the Firefighters Calendar fund-raiser. Omar was one of the firemen featured in the calendar. And his picture…Gabrielle could stare at all day.

Shirtless, with his suspenders pulled over his shoulders, Omar was standing on the fire truck's ladder. One arm was outstretched over his head and gripping one of the ladder rungs, causing his bicep to bulge. His body was gleaming with sweat.

And what a body… Those six-pack abs. The hard grooves and planes. He was in amazing shape.

Suddenly, Gabrielle was thinking about what Pauline had said. About letting go and having some fun.

Looking at Omar now, she knew that he would certainly be fun to play with.

Gabrielle got up from her desk and walked away from the computer. She couldn't believe the thought going through her mind. Since when was she this kind of person?

And yet, Pauline had made it clear that a casual relationship had helped her get over Steve.

Gabrielle returned to her desk. Shamelessly, she continued to study the photo of Omar…every beautiful inch of him.

What did other people think of the photos? She scrolled down to the bottom of the article, to the comments section.

OMG, these firefighters are so hot!

I love a man who is strong enough to pull you from a burning building. {{dreamy sigh}}

Good Lord. Omar is F-I-N-E! Is there anything hotter than a man in suspenders and his fire gear?

I hear all of these guys are single. I wouldn't kick any of them out of my bed anytime soon. Especially not Omar…

And on went the comments. Clearly, women loved a man in uniform…or in this case, a man partially dressed in uniform. Was the uniform getting to her as well, the whole firefighter fantasy?

"Good grief, Gabby," she said to herself. "You don't need a man to save you. You can take care of yourself."

Pauline's words came back to her then. *Every woman needs a guy to rock her world once in a while. Know what I'm saying?*

Maybe that's what this firefighter fantasy was all about. Knowing that these strong men were capable of taking care of you in the bedroom…

Gabrielle closed her laptop. Something was seriously wrong with her. Was she actually thinking of having sex—

She stopped the thought before it fully formed. Then she went to the kitchen and poured herself a glass of water.

Pauline had been frank with her, and Gabrielle had expected nothing less. Maybe there *was* a dark cloud hanging over her. And she could concede that it had to do with more than her parents' restaurant being burned down.

Gabrielle was lonely. And it was something she hadn't allowed herself to consider until Pauline had forced her to face the facts.

She missed having someone in bed with her at night. And not just for the physical intimacy, but the emotional intimacy as well.

"Why am I still thinking about this?" Gabrielle asked herself.

It was Pauline and her inquisition—and unexpected encouragement—that had Gabrielle's mind tracking in one direction right now. And the more she thought about it, the more frustrated she got.

Because no matter what Pauline said, Gabrielle couldn't get involved with a man she knew was a player. She just didn't have it in her.

So even if she had nights when she was totally lonely, she could deal with it. Unlike some of those ogling women who had commented about Omar's body, Gabrielle could exercise some self-control.

Just because she was attracted to someone didn't mean she had to act on that attraction.

A one-night stand wasn't her style.

Never would be.

Omar dropped the pen down on the report he had just finished writing and leaned back in his chair. His eyes went to his cell phone resting on the desk. He stared at it as though it were a ticking time bomb.

Reaching forward, he snatched it up. And though he knew he wouldn't find anything, he checked it nonetheless. Maybe he'd missed a message when they'd been out at the scene of the car accident.

He scrolled through his text messages. But that action only confirmed what he already knew.

Gabrielle hadn't called him. She hadn't texted.

Frowning, Omar twirled the phone end over end.

She'd said she would call if there was a problem, so not hearing from her was good news. It meant she hadn't found any cause for concern. However, Omar had hoped that she would simply call him. Maybe send him a text to say hi.

He just wanted to hear from her.

He had last seen her on Friday night, and the cable station didn't air any new programming on the weekend. Yes, he'd checked. So a trip to the station to pop in and visit her would have been futile.

Now, it was Sunday evening. And he had spent the past two days thinking about her.

Well, he had spent the past two days trying *not* to think of her. But even a Saturday night out at a bar with his friends hadn't taken his thoughts off her. One of his buddies from another firehouse had noticed that he wasn't quite himself. He had shown no interest in talking to any of the women who were trying to get his attention.

Omar knew what it was like to walk into a room and turn heads. To have women desperate to spend time with him. So why was it that Gabrielle wanted nothing to do with him?

The alarm began to blare. "Truck fourteen, engine twenty-one. Structure fire at 299 Orleans Avenue."

Instantly, Omar dropped his phone and raced to get into his turnout gear along with his colleagues. Another restaurant fire?

And sure enough, it was.

The arsonist wasn't letting up.

On Monday morning, right after Gabrielle had poured herself her first cup of coffee, Janine the station manager hurried into her office.

"What's up?" Gabrielle asked, alarmed.

"Just got word from one of my sources. A man was admitted to hospital last night with burns on his hands and arms. And as you know, there was another restaurant fire last night. A Korean place. This could be the arsonist."

Gabrielle perked up instantly. "Where?"

"Ocean City General."

Adrenaline pumped through Gabrielle's veins. She needed to go over there. "What's his condition?"

"I don't have answers yet. But my source said he would

get back to me as soon as possible." Janine's eyes lit up. "It might be nothing, or it might be everything."

"Tell me something as soon as you know," Gabrielle said.

Omar's phone began to ring. His eyes popped open, and for a moment he was disoriented. He glanced at his bedside clock, saw that it was 9:32 a.m.. He'd barely gotten home from his shift and fallen asleep.

He reached for the phone. And his heart began to pound when he saw a number he didn't recognize flashing on his screen. Gabrielle?

He quickly answered the call. "Hello?" he said groggily.

"Omar, hi. It's Gabrielle."

He was about to give her a proper greeting when she continued speaking. "There's a man who's been admitted to Ocean City General. He has burns on his hands and arms. He could be the arsonist. I need you to—"

"Whoa," Omar said. "Slow down."

"Sorry—did I wake you up?"

"I just finished my twenty-four-hour shift."

"Oh. I didn't know."

"It's okay." Omar sat up. "What's this you're saying about the arsonist?"

"A Korean restaurant burned down last night."

"Yeah, I know. I was there."

"Someone was admitted to Ocean City General with burns on his arms and hands. This could be the guy."

"He will be investigated, I assure you."

"I need to be able to see him," Gabrielle said. "If I see him, I'll know if this was the guy who was at the scene of the fire last week."

"Is that why you're calling me? To see if I can get you in to see him?"

"I've been sitting here for forty minutes since I heard the news, and I already feel like I'm going crazy. I feel so anxious about it. I just need to know. And I'm the one who can identify him."

"Hold up," Omar said. "You expect hospital staff to just let you visit him?"

"Not if *I* called them, no. But I'm sure you can make it happen."

Omar was annoyed. This was why she was calling him? He'd made it clear to her that he wanted to get to know her, and she was only calling him now when she needed something? "I can't help you."

"Sure you can," Gabrielle said.

"You really sound like you're used to getting your way. You snap a finger, and things get done. It must be killing you that you have to sit back and wait for results here. But that's exactly what you're going to have to do. There is a protocol for this, and I can assure you that the police will be looking into this person. Looking for facts to determine whether or not he is possibly the arsonist."

"But—"

"The best I can do is make some calls, see what I can find out. But I won't be doing that until I get some sleep."

There was silence on the other end of the line.

"You know, I was really hoping you would have called me for another reason. Not just when you need something like this and think I can help you." He sounded testy in his own ears. "I'll touch base with you later."

Gabrielle felt like a jerk. Omar's tone said it all. He felt as if she was using him.

Yes, she had hoped that he could help her. But she'd

also wanted to share the news with him. Once she'd learned about the possible arsonist being admitted to hospital, she'd been excited and wanted to let him know. But she'd deliberately spoken to him in a way to make it sound as if her calling him was all business.

According to Pauline, Gabrielle wore an emotional brick wall to keep everyone out. And how she'd just treated Omar…she knew it was an attempt to keep him out.

The truth was, she was far too attracted to him. That attraction scared her.

So she sent him a quick text saying, I was a jerk. I'm sorry. Get some rest. I'll talk to you later.

Omar looked at the computer screen—and finally he understood.

For the life of him, he hadn't been able to understand why Gabrielle could turn him down so easily. Not when there was definitely chemistry between them. No matter how hard he tried, he couldn't put her out of his mind. So today, after her call, he'd decided to search the internet for stories about her.

And what he found… It was enlightening.

And enraging.

As Omar read the article that explained everything, he fumed. Why hadn't Gabrielle just told him the truth? Why give him the line about "knowing his type" and not being interested?

The truth was much easier for him to accept, even though he didn't like it. She was engaged to be married. No wonder she had been over-the-top cold with him.

He hadn't noticed a ring. Naw, she couldn't have been wearing one. He would have seen that. Maybe she was the type of woman who didn't want to wear expensive jewelry at work. Or, knowing her, she probably thought wearing an engagement ring was an entirely sexist practice.

Yeah, that was more like it.

He wondered why she had kissed him at all.

Couldn't she have just told him that she was involved with someone? Almost ready to walk down the aisle, for goodness' sake? That would've at least answered things for him. He wouldn't have bothered to go back to see her. Wouldn't have kissed her.

Omar tipped his head back, realization dawning. No wonder she hadn't wanted him to follow her home. That would have been hard to explain to her fiancé.

Omar gritted his teeth. Man.

Again, he looked at the picture of Gabrielle and her fiancé on his computer screen. They had gotten engaged a year ago Valentine's Day. Omar had never seen the guy before. He was a good-looking dude. Tall. And Gabrielle seemed happy in his arms, which made his blood boil even more.

Chill out, he told himself. *She's not your girl, man. So what if you're rejected? You can't have them all.*

That's what he told himself. But it didn't make him feel better. Not one bit.

And as five o'clock rolled around, Omar knew that he was going to head to the cable station.

Gabrielle owed him an explanation.

Chapter 13

Omar got out of his vehicle when he saw Gabrielle round the sidewalk into the parking lot area. He stepped from between the parked cars, and saw her halt as she looked in his direction.

He wanted to be livid. He wanted to feel nothing when he looked at her except anger. But again, there was that pull of attraction, stronger than ever.

Man, she looked good. She was wearing a dark pink dress that hugged her curves. Matching pink pumps. Her long legs looked delectable. And the dark sunglasses she wore made her look chic as well as sexy.

Omar swallowed. He wanted nothing more than to go over to her, pull her close and kiss her again. Kiss her until she told him that she didn't really love this other guy. Because how could this woman who had him riled up for the first time in ages belong to someone else?

She pushed her sunglasses up into her shoulder-length

hair, a tentative smile coming onto her lips. Of course—
now she was giving him a warm reception.

Now that he knew she belonged to another man.

She walked toward him saying, "Omar. I didn't expect
to see you. Did you find out something about the guy admitted to hospital?"

"Why didn't you tell me? Why did you let me carry
on like a fool?"

Omar saw the look of befuddlement in Gabrielle's eyes.
"Tell you what?"

He laughed without mirth. "Are we going to play this
game? You made it seem as though you weren't attracted
to me, as though you hated my very character. That that
was the reason you wouldn't give me the time of day. All
you had to do was tell me you were engaged."

He watched her carefully. Saw those beautiful eyes
widen. For a moment, she looked confused. Then realization dawned.

"I looked you up on the internet," Omar said. "Should've
done that beforehand, just to spare myself the embarrass-
ment. You could have at least been forthcoming."

"Can we talk about this in my car? Or yours? I have
colleagues exiting the building—"

"Sure," Omar said, sarcasm in his tone. "We can take
your feelings into consideration."

"Omar…"

"This is my vehicle," he said, motioning to his car.

Gabrielle walked briskly to the passenger side of his
car, and Omar wondered why he was even there. She was
engaged. End of story. He'd learned the truth on his own.
He didn't need her to confirm it for him.

But he wanted her to. Wanted to know why she had
let him hit on her without once telling him that she was
off the market.

Or maybe the truth was that he wanted to see her one last time...

When Omar got into the car beside her, she faced him. "First of all," she began, "I don't have to have an excuse not to want to go out with you."

"You kissed me," Omar said.

"*You* kissed *me*," she countered.

"You were a willing participant."

She laughed, but the sound held no humor. "You have got to be the most arrogant—"

"Why didn't you tell me?" Omar demanded.

He saw her jaw flinch, and almost thought she wasn't going to answer him. But then she said, "I didn't tell you because I'm not engaged."

Confused, he stared at her. He didn't understand. "What do you mean?"

"I'm not engaged, Omar."

Hearing it a second time, Omar's heart began to beat erratically. Excitement began to course through him, hot and sweet.

"But I saw the articles," he said, not quite ready to believe her. "You got engaged last Valentine's Day."

"And by the summer, he was sleeping with my cousin and things were over."

She spoke flippantly, as though what she'd endured had been no big deal. But maybe—finally—it explained everything. "You're telling me the truth?"

"Why would I lie?" Gabrielle asked. She drew in a deep breath. "So, there you go. That's why I'm not engaged anymore."

She shrugged nonchalantly, though Omar knew that she could not feel nonchalant about such a devastating betrayal. "I'm sorry," he found himself saying. "Any guy who would cheat on you has got to be the world's biggest moron."

"Apparently, he's very happy now."

"Meaning what? That you couldn't make him happy?"

Gabrielle shrugged, but didn't meet his eyes.

"Hey," Omar said softly. "You can't believe that."

He saw her swallow. "I don't want to talk about this."

"Is he the reason you're pushing me away? Because you're still in love with him?"

Gabrielle made a face. "God no."

He rested his arm on the car's console, leaning closer to her. "You're single. So am I. And when we kissed, there was something there. If it's not someone else you're involved with, why do you keep pushing me away?"

Gabrielle said nothing.

"And don't tell me that there's nothing between us. Because even when I touched you…" He stroked her face, and as he looked at her, he saw the slight quiver of her bottom lip. "Yes," he said, the word almost a sigh. "You felt something then. You're feeling it now. God, I want to kiss you again."

Her lips parted, and he almost expected her to protest as she had before. But when he saw how her eyes had darkened with lust, he ran the pad of his thumb along her bottom lip.

A sigh escaped her mouth.

Leaning forward, he pressed his nose against her cheek. He felt her tremble. And he knew without a doubt that he was right about the connection between them.

"Don't make me believe I'm crazy," he told her. "Tell me you feel this, too."

"You are crazy," she told him. But her words didn't hold any conviction. Easing back, he looked into her eyes.

She had an undeniable look of longing on her face. Longing to be kissed. Touched.

"Am I crazy now?" he asked, and planted a soft kiss at the corner of her mouth.

"Oh, God."

His groin tightened. He was barely touching her, yet the way she was responding...

"What if I do this?" he asked, and kissed her on the mouth briefly.

She moved forward when he broke the kiss, telling him that she wanted more.

"And will you tell me I'm crazy if I do this?" Pushing her hair back, he brought his lips to her ear and gently pulled the lobe between his teeth. Then he eased back.

"No," she rasped. "You're not crazy."

A smile pulled at Omar's lips. *Finally.*

Framing her cheeks with both of his hands, he brought his lips down on hers. Fire filled him instantly, as hot as any blaze he had fought while in uniform. He kissed her, his tongue delving deep into her mouth. He slipped his fingers into her hair, holding her close and not wanting to let her go.

She mewled softly, and it was his undoing. Omar deepened the kiss. He wanted to be inside her. He needed it.

When he heard the ringing phone, he was instantly disoriented. For a moment, he was snapped out of a place of fantasy and confused about what was going on.

"That's my phone," Gabrielle said.

"Let it ring," he said, and started to kiss her again.

"I can't... I have to answer it."

He groaned as she broke the kiss and reached into the purse on her lap. She pulled out her phone and swiped to answer it. "Mom?"

Omar heard the frantic screaming on the other end of the line.

"Slow down, Mom. What's going on?" As she listened, her face fell. "Oh, my God, Mom. I'm on my way. I'm on my way right now."

Omar looked at her with concern as she lowered the phone from her ear. "What is it, Gabrielle?"

"It's my father," she said, sounding breathless and scared. "He's had a second heart attack. I have to go to Saint Peter's Hospital right now."

She reached for the door handle, but in her haste, didn't quite open it. Her breathing was becoming more ragged by the second.

"Stay in the car," Omar told her.

"I have to go to the hospital."

"You're in no condition to drive. I'll take you there."

Gabrielle was gripped by fear as Omar drove her to the hospital. Her heart pounded the entire way there. She was terrified, but she knew she had to do her best to keep it together.

"Why are we getting every single traffic light?" she asked in frustration.

"We're almost there," Omar told her. "I wish I could have the lights and sirens going for you, but I can't."

Minutes later, Omar was pulling into the emergency bay of the hospital. Gabrielle started opening the door before the car was even stopped.

"Thank you," she said.

"I'll go in with you."

He drove up about twenty feet, parking in front of an ambulance. Gabrielle was vaguely aware of him greeting the ambulance driver as he came around to meet her at the back of his vehicle. He put an arm around her shoulder as they walked to the entrance. She was glad he was there, because her legs felt like Jell-O and she feared they wouldn't hold her.

As they stepped into the waiting room, Gabrielle glanced around frantically. She heard her mother before she saw her. The wail came from the other side of the room, and when Gabrielle looked in that direction, she saw her mother jumping to her feet.

"Mom!" Gabrielle exclaimed. She rushed toward her mother, while her mother hurried toward her. Meeting each other, they hugged and cried.

"I only went downstairs for a minute," Gina sobbed. "I went to make him some tea, and when I went back up to the room—"

"It's not your fault, Mom. But please, tell me how bad it was."

"I don't know yet," Gina said.

"Okay," Gabrielle said, making sure to speak evenly. If they were working on him, that meant he wasn't dead. "Was he taking his medication?"

"It's been so hard."

"That doesn't answer the question." Gabrielle took her mother by the shoulders and looked her in the eye. "Has he been taking his medication?"

"He said he doesn't want to live this way."

"Oh, dear God." Gabrielle felt as if *she* was about to have a heart attack, herself. Had her father actually stopped taking his medication?

Hugging her torso, Gabrielle turned. And there was Omar. He was looking at her with sympathy and concern. "How bad is it?" he asked.

"I don't know." Gabrielle shook her head. "I don't know," she repeated, her voice cracking with emotion.

Her mother was so distraught that she didn't even ask

Gabrielle who Omar was. "Mom, go back and have a seat. I have to say goodbye to a friend who brought me here."

Gina wandered off, sobbing softly.

Looking up at Omar, Gabrielle said, "Omar, I'm going to be here for a while. I'll get a taxi back to the station to pick up my car."

"I can stay with you if you like."

Gabrielle shook her head. "It's going to be awkward. I'm here for my mother, and she's here for me."

"Can I pick you up something to eat?"

She shook her head. "I can't eat anything. Not now."

"Call me," Omar said. "If you need me to pick you up. Or if you need me for any reason at all."

She looked up at him and smiled though her heart was breaking. "Thank you."

Omar pulled her into his arms and planted a kiss on her forehead while giving her a warm hug. "I'm a phone call away, okay?"

"Okay," Gabrielle replied, her voice faint.

Releasing her, Omar turned and walked out of the waiting room. Gabrielle watched him go before she went to sit with her mother.

"Oh, sweetie," Gina whimpered. "I can't lose him!"

Gabrielle held her mother, tears filling her eyes. She couldn't hold them back now. She couldn't lose her father either…

But good grief, was he trying to die?

"He's just so stressed out," Gina said as if in response to Gabrielle's unspoken question. "He's angry. He's so bitter about what happened."

"I know it's upsetting," Gabrielle began, "but Daddy still has a lot to live for. The arsonist didn't take what was most important. But if Dad dies because of this… We will lose everything. And the arsonist will win. Mom, if you guys can't rebuild or if you don't want to, that's okay. You've worked so hard all of your lives. Maybe this is the time you're supposed to just be relaxing and enjoying life. Take a cruise. Go on a tour of China. Go to Europe. Enjoy each other."

"I know, honey. You're right."

Gabrielle's voice broke. "I want you to be happy. You and Daddy have worked so hard, and you did well in life. Now you deserve to take it easy and enjoy yourselves."

Gina said nothing. She could only cry. Gabrielle held her mother's hand and leaned her shoulder against hers. All they could do was be there for each other as they waited.

Chapter 14

Much later, Joe's cardiologist, a man named Dr. Ivanovich, came out to see Gabrielle and her mother. He delivered the bad news.

"Joe has indeed had another heart attack. I was hoping it was just chest pain, a false alarm. We can no longer ignore the fact that his coronary artery disease is going to require surgery. His best chance of survival is to have a triple bypass."

Gina threw a hand to her mouth. "No."

"For now, we have him on medications to alleviate the pain and the symptoms. He's getting oxygen. But we're going to need to schedule a family meeting to discuss his surgery, and what needs to take place."

Gina whimpered. Gabrielle put her arm around her mother's shoulders and hugged her close. Then she asked the doctor, "Can we see him?"

"Yes," Dr. Ivanovich said. "Follow me."

They followed the doctor into the area where the emergency patients were held. The only privacy afforded to the beds were thin drapes you pulled around them.

When Gabrielle saw her father, she wanted to cry. He looked fragile, and so sad. His life seemed to be ebbing away from him.

Her father offered her a weak smile. "I'm sorry, Gabby," he said as she reached his bedside.

She took his hand. "Daddy, I love you."

"I don't think we can go back to running the restaurant, darling," he said.

"Who cares about the restaurant?" Gabrielle asked. "You can't kill yourself. What's Mom gonna do? What am I going to do?" She looked at him, and waited for an answer, but he didn't say anything. He didn't have to. "Look, I know you think you lost everything because of the arsonist. And I'm determined to do what I can to see him caught. But I said to Mom earlier that maybe… Maybe this is for the best."

Joe's eyes widened as he looked at her. "For the best? How can you say that?"

"Because everything happens for a reason. I have to believe that. Sometimes, things happen that we don't like. But if you search, you can find the reason why. And I think that in your case, the reason is that it's finally time for you and Mom to take a break. You both worked so hard your entire lives. Running a restaurant isn't easy. Before the arsonist struck, you were already stressed. You had to put in a ton of hours. That's what's necessary to make a go of a restaurant. I know you did it for Mom, because this was her dream. But you know what… Her bigger dream is to have you around."

Joe's eyes went from his daughter to his wife. His face twisted with emotion.

"She's right," Gina said. "I always wanted this restaurant, but I don't need it."

"You deserve it," Joe said.

"I want my husband more."

His eyes misted. He knew this was a losing argument.

"No more missing your medication. No more arguing about the food you need to eat. I'm not going to let you die on me."

"It's all those green leafy vegetables that are going to kill me," Joe said.

Gabrielle shook her head. Even now, her father was being stubborn. "Daddy, if that's your way of saying you're not going to change your diet, then we're going to have a *big* problem."

"Gabby suggested we should be traveling," Gina said, taking her husband's hand. "Enjoying our retirement. And she's right."

"But I wanted to give you your dream." Joe's face contorted with pain. "All these years, you were there with me. You put off your dreams because we wanted to accomplish other things."

"Like raising a family," Gina said. "We did that." She looked at Gabrielle. "And we did it well. I have no regrets."

"For decades, all you ever wanted to do was run a restaurant."

"Joe, you have given me my dream every day I have been married to you. As for the restaurant, you even gave me that dream. I had it for six months. But I don't need it. That's what I'm telling you. I need my husband."

"Daddy, this is the time to relax after all the hard work you've done," Gabrielle said. "You don't need to work so hard anymore."

Gabrielle knew her father would have a hard time comprehending her words. All Joe Leonard knew was hard work.

But that was going to have to change and fast.

Gina raised Joe's hand to her lips and kissed it. "I can't lose the only man I've ever loved."

Joe smiled through his tear-filled eyes. "Oh, sweetheart. I love you, too."

"Then live for me, darling. Because I can't live my life without you."

Gabrielle wanted to stay at the hospital with her parents, but her father insisted that she leave. So did her mother. They both assured her that he would be fine, and of course, Gabrielle would visit the next day.

The family meeting was also scheduled for tomorrow afternoon. Gabrielle would be able to go to the studio, tape her show then leave. Obviously, her father needed her right now.

Omar had texted her a couple times during the evening to see how things were going and if she was okay. He again even offered to pick her up. But considering Gabrielle didn't leave the hospital until after eleven, she'd decided it was best to take a cab to get her car.

When she got home shortly before midnight, she texted Omar to tell him she was going to bed and that she would talk to him tomorrow.

She was emotionally drained. But she was also relieved. At least for now, her father was okay. His cardiologist was renowned, and Gabrielle trusted that he would take the best care of her father.

While Gabrielle had gone home for the night, her mother, of course, was going to stay at the hospital with her husband. Her parents had held hands the entire time in the hospital emergency area, only releasing each other when her father was being transferred to his permanent room. But once upstairs in his new bed, her mother resumed her post at his side, once again holding the hand of the man she loved.

It made Gabrielle miss that in her life. That special connection with someone.

She was thirty-five. She didn't want to grow old and never experience that kind of love. The in-sickness-and-in-health kind of love.

Maybe Pauline was right. She should make it her New Year's resolution to meet a potential love interest.

Maybe she had already met him…

Gabrielle snuggled under the covers and tried not to think about her father or Omar. Because tonight, she needed to get some rest.

Gabrielle got more rest than she expected, out of sheer exhaustion. She got to the station forty-five minutes earlier than she normally did. She needed to get an early start to her day. Because the family meeting with the cardiologist was this afternoon, she was going to have to leave work a little early. One of the special features segment hosts might have to take over for her a couple of days this week, depending on when her father's surgery would be scheduled and how things went.

The thing about being on television, you couldn't have a bad day. Gabrielle had mastered the skill of performing—making it look to the audience as though she didn't have a care in the world. But once the show was taped, she felt depleted. She wished she could head straight to the hospital to see her father, but there were a few things she needed to do before she could leave.

She called her mother once she was back in the office. "Hi, Mom. How's Daddy?"

"He's good. He's listening to his nurses, eating what they give him. We're already talking about planning a European cruise for when he's better," Gina added. Gabrielle could hear a smile in her voice.

"That's great," Gabrielle said. "I'll see you soon. I just have to do a couple of things first."

"I called Grace," Gina said. "But I couldn't reach her."

"I'll give her a call," Gabrielle said.

An hour later, Gabrielle was finally heading out of her office. "Give your father my love," Janine said to her as she was on her way out.

"Thanks, Janine. I will."

Once Gabrielle got to her car, she called her sister. Something she hadn't done in years.

"Grace," Gabrielle began without preamble when her sister answered the phone. "You need to come home."

"Hello to you, too," Grace said.

"Grace, I don't have time to get into it with you. Dad had another heart attack."

For a moment, there was silence on the other end of the line. Then, Gabrielle heard a gasp. "Tell me you're lying."

"I wish I were," Gabrielle said. "You should have gotten yourself down here already," she couldn't help saying, "but now that he's had another heart attack, you have to. He's going to have surgery, a triple bypass. We could… We could lose him."

"Oh, my God."

"Just tell me that you're coming."

"My finances are tight right now."

"Are you kidding me—"

"But I'll get there," Grace said. "I will."

"You'd better," Gabrielle told her. "Mom needs you, Dad needs you." She refrained from saying that she needed her. Because she was too upset with her sister that she wouldn't let herself.

But she *did* want her sister back. She wanted her sister back *whole*. No more alcohol, no more drugs. The responsible girl who lived inside of Grace—that's who Gabrielle wanted.

"Let me know when you're on your way," Gabrielle said.

Then she ended the call and headed straight to the hospital.

Shortly after seven p.m., Omar saw Gabrielle's number flashing on his screen. He dropped the wooden spoon into the pot of pasta sauce and answered the call. "Hello?"

He heard her soft groan on the other end of the line. "Hi."

"Are you okay?" Omar asked.

"Can I see you?" she asked, her voice sounding small.

"Absolutely," Omar told her. "You want me to meet you somewhere?"

"Actually... How would you feel about coming here? To my place? I just... I need to talk to someone."

Omar turned off the stove. "I was just making some dinner. It's almost finished, so I can come after that. Have you eaten?"

"Okay."

"Have you eaten?" he asked.

"No."

"I'm making pasta Bolognese with pork. Is that good for you? If not, I can pick up something else."

"No, that's totally fine. I'm not sure I can eat much, anyway."

"I'll pack up the food and head right over. What's your address?"

Chapter 15

Gabrielle's shoulders drooped with relief when she opened the door and saw Omar standing there. "Hi," she said to him.

He smiled down at her. "Hey."

"Thanks for coming. I hope… I hope I didn't pull you away from something important."

"Naw. I'm happy to come and see you." He lifted a tote bag. "I brought pasta and garlic bread. I also stopped to pick up some wine."

"Thank you."

Then she stood back, opening the door wide so that Omar could enter.

He glanced around. "I like it," he said. "It's like you. Efficient."

"What does that mean?"

"You seem fairly no-nonsense, so I didn't expect you to have an over-the-top house. This is nice. Beautifully decorated, no clutter. I'm impressed."

"I hate clutter. I have enough clutter in my brain, I don't need to look around and see it."

Omar began walking toward her kitchen. It wasn't large, but it was efficient, as he had said. A breakfast bar provided the casual seating as well as extra counter space. And she had lots of cupboards so she didn't need to have excess items muddling up her counters.

"Whatever you brought smells delicious," Gabrielle said. Her stomach was grumbling in response to the tantalizing smells.

Omar went over to her electric stove, where he placed the tote bag. Then he began to take the items out of the bag. He withdrew a large plastic container, which she could see contained salad. Then he withdrew a fairly sizable thermos travel bag. Within that were two more containers.

"I don't know if you like this brand," he said, passing her a bottle of red wine that was also in the tote bag.

"It's perfect," she told him.

Gabrielle went to the cupboard to get two wineglasses, and also to take out some plates. When she went back over to Omar, she saw the large container of pasta noodles with meat sauce. He'd even packed Parmesan cheese. Another container held garlic bread. The smells were an assault on her senses.

"Everything should still be warm."

"Did you make all of this?" she asked.

"Well, not the wine nor the Parmesan cheese."

"So you can cook?" That was certainly an attractive trait in a man. Tobias hadn't even been able to boil water.

"I cook at the firehouse all the time," he told her. "Actually, a lot of us can cook pretty well. We're used to cooking large family meals for when we all sit down and eat together."

"That sounds nice." Except for the times she went out with Pauline, or went to her parents' for dinner, Gabrielle ate at home alone. Which meant she didn't do too much eating. Typically, she picked up something from the grocery store, like a roasted chicken or prepackaged meal from the hot foods section. Something quick. And the times she didn't feel like doing that, she came home and made toast with peanut butter, or a quick soup. She didn't spend too much time making home-cooked meals for one.

Her first thought had been to set up the plates at the breakfast bar, but then she decided to bring them to her dining room table. It would be nice to use it for a change.

Then she went back over to Omar. "Let's just bring everything to the table, and we can share it there."

She found her corkscrew, and opened the wine. Then she brought the bottle and the two glasses to the table. Omar had just finished setting down the container with the salad. "I've already tossed it with a vinaigrette dressing. I hope that's okay."

"Everything smells scrumptious. Trust me, I'm looking forward to sitting down and using this dining room table for a home-cooked meal."

As she sat, Omar gave her an odd look. "You don't cook?"

"Usually, I'm so tired by the time I get home from the studio that I either just pick something up on the way, or I make something quick."

"That's not good."

"Besides, it's only me. I can't be bothered to make an elaborate meal for one person."

Omar nodded. "I'm glad I can help you put this table to use, then." He gestured to the food. "Ladies first."

Gabrielle lifted the container with salad and put some

onto her plate. Then she did the same with the pasta. But the first thing she sampled was the garlic bread, because the delicious aroma kept wafting into her nose and teasing her belly. One bite, and she was in heaven. "You made this? From scratch?"

"I bought the bread. But I seasoned it, yeah."

"Oh, my goodness." It was cheesy and delicious. "This is phenomenal."

Omar smiled. "If you think that's amazing, I can't wait for you to taste the pasta."

Gabrielle put the bread at the side of her plate and used her fork to twirl up some of the pasta Bolognese. And when she tasted it, her eyes fluttered shut. She chewed— no, savored—and then swallowed before speaking. "Wow. Where did you learn to cook such amazing food?"

Omar chuckled softly. "I learned at the firehouse."

No wonder women fantasized over firefighters. If this was how they could cook…

She was ravenous as she ate. This was the best meal she had had in ages, and she ate a second full helping. It was as though she hadn't eaten in years. Omar couldn't help but comment.

"I have to say," he began, "I love a girl who knows how to eat."

"You think I ate too much?"

Omar waved off the suggestion. "Not at all. In fact, why do I get the sense that you don't eat enough?"

"My best friend would agree with you. She tells me that I drink too much coffee, don't eat enough decent meals. It's on my list of New Year's resolutions to take a cooking class. Or to just get reacquainted with my kitchen," she said and smiled.

"Well, we have to do something about that."

Gabrielle's eyes caught Omar's. She wondered if he

was suggesting that he teach her how to cook. Or perhaps that they just spend more time together sharing meals.

Either idea was appealing because it meant spending more time with him.

She didn't know why, but him being here with her felt right. At least for the moment, she'd had an escape from the headache of worrying about her father. She enjoyed a decent meal, and decent company.

And he didn't seem at all like the bad guy she'd tried so hard to make him out to be.

In fact, with everything he did, he was proving he was a good guy.

Gabrielle sipped her wine and told herself not to get ahead of herself. For right now at least, she was open to the possibility of something happening with Omar. As Pauline had said, she didn't have to think about her next fiancé or forever. But Omar would certainly be good enough to scratch the itch that was becoming more intense the more time she spent with him.

"Unfortunately, I didn't get to bring any dessert," Omar said.

"You can probably make your own homemade ice cream, can't you?" Gabrielle joked.

"Actually, I have a great blender. You can make ice cream in it."

"You're kidding me."

"Nope. You can make smoothies, soups, ice cream. A whole variety of healthy stuff."

"How is that possible?" Gabrielle asked.

"If you come to my place, I can show you."

At the mere suggestion of her going to his place, Gabrielle's heart began beating a little faster. No doubt about it, she could imagine getting naked with him...

Would it really be wrong to act on what she was feeling? To be like other women who went after what they wanted?

She pushed her chair back and stood. "I've got a couple ice cream bars in the fridge. Want one for dessert?"

"Sure thing."

A short while later, Gabrielle led Omar to her living room. She sat on the sofa, and he sat beside her. During dinner, they hadn't spoken about what was bothering her—the reason she had asked him to come and join her. But now, Omar wanted to know more.

"What's going on?" he asked. "You sounded pretty upset when you called me, but I figure if your father had taken a turn for the worst, you would have said so by now."

"No, he's stable."

"Thank God," Omar said. "That's great to hear."

"Yes, thank God. But I'm scared," she admitted.

Omar was seeing a completely different side of her tonight. The strong, feisty woman wasn't in the room now. She was pleasant, vulnerable. And it brought out his protective instincts.

All he wanted to do was hold her and make all of her problems go away.

"He's going to have to have triple bypass surgery," Gabrielle told him. "I'm terrified. Every surgery carries risk, but this one… There was a meeting at the hospital today, and they're getting my father in for the surgery as soon as possible. Friday."

"That's fast," Omar commented. "Three days from now."

"The fact that they've scheduled the surgery so quickly is something that also worries me. It must mean they feel his condition is really grave."

Omar knew there was no point in sugarcoating the situation, and he was certain that Gabrielle was not the type of woman who deluded herself. "This is a second heart attack within several weeks, right?"

"Yes," she said. Her voice sounded meek, so unlike the brazen woman he had first met.

"Then I'm sure they believe the situation is grave." When her eyes widened, he quickly continued. "But the excellent thing is that they're acting swiftly. I think your father's gonna be okay. If he could hang on after two heart attacks...he's got fight in him. As you know, some people have a heart attack and don't make it. I see a lot of that as a firefighter."

"I guess you do. I guess you see a lot of awful things."

"Yeah," Omar said. "Not just fires. We respond to car crashes, industrial accidents...it can get ugly. And I'm on the rescue squad, so I've seen even more harrowing situations."

"I saw online that you saved a boy last month. Just before Christmas. The one who fell in a well."

A smile touched Omar's lips. "Yeah. That's always the best feeling. When you can save a life. You know you've made a huge difference."

"How do you handle it? The sight of blood makes me feel queasy. How do you deal with seeing severely injured victims?"

Omar sipped his own wine. "That's the hardest part," he admitted. "And it never gets easy. But you have to find a way to block it out. I do that by concentrating on *saving* a life, rather than thinking about the fact that someone might be dying."

"I'm impressed. Mentally, you have to be really strong to see tragedy day after day and still be able to function." Gabrielle reached for her wine, and took a sip. She looked at him with a little smile. "Why did you go into firefighting?"

"It's a bit of a long story. In fact, my parents still ask me that question today." He chuckled softly.

"What do you mean?"

"My parents have a very successful business. They started a cookie company twenty years ago. One flavor, but it sold like wildfire. The golden chocolate chip cookie."

"Are you kidding me? I love that cookie!"

"Well, that was my mother's secret recipe when we were young. At some point, she decided to start a business. It started small, home orders at first. Then business orders. Then it led to a factory and going statewide. Now, they sell nationally."

"That's incredible," Gabrielle said. "I guess your mother and my mother have something in common. My mother always wanted to go to culinary school. She made the most amazing meals, but she just couldn't afford to pursue her dream of being a chef. That's why she and my father opened this restaurant last year. After so many years of working hard and sacrificing, my mother was finally doing the one thing she'd always wanted to do. And then the arsonist stole that from them."

Omar saw the pain streak across Gabrielle's face, and he wished desperately that he could take away her pain. "I'm really sorry."

"It's just so hard. But I tried to tell my father last night that no matter how much he feels he lost because of the arsonist, he still has what matters most. His life, and my mother."

"Hopefully, he can concentrate on that," Omar said. "That'll pull him through."

"Hopefully the second heart attack will be his wake-up call," Gabrielle said, and made a sour face. "My dad wasn't taking his medications as he should have been. He's been fighting my mother over eating healthy food. That's what led to the second heart attack. We could have lost him…"

Omar edged closer to her on the sofa and took her hand in his. It felt like the right thing to do. "I know it's overwhelming. But anytime you want to talk, or you want a nice home-cooked meal… I'm here."

"Some days, I feel so alone in all of this."

"Do you have a sister or brother?"

"A sister," Gabrielle said. "But she's living in Portland."

She sipped her wine, and Omar got the sense that there was more going on there. "You two get along?" he asked.

Twirling the stem of her wineglass between her fingers, Gabrielle shook her head. "Nope. We don't."

Omar waited for her to continue. But her lips pulled into a tight line.

"Why don't you get along?" he asked. He wanted her to get what she needed to off her chest.

"It's not because I don't want to get along with her," Gabrielle continued. "But…she's always been irresponsible. My parents have made excuses upon excuses for her. And I did for a long time, too. I've bailed her out with more money than I can count after one crisis in her life after another. Finally, it clicked that if I was always coming to her rescue, she'd never learn to take care of herself. So I told her I wouldn't do it anymore. She wasn't happy with me, to say the least. Our relationship since that point has been really tense."

"How long has that been?" Omar asked.

"A few years."

"That's tough. I have a brother and a sister. I don't see them much, because they relocated to Texas with my parents, where they opened up the cookie factory. They're both heavily involved with the family business."

"And you never went with them?" Gabrielle narrowed her eyes with curiosity.

"No. I stayed here and… I became a firefighter."

Omar had stayed for Mika. But he had lost her. Then, he had thrown himself into becoming a firefighter. It was the one thing he could do to make himself feel empowered. Being able to save other lives, when he'd lost the woman he'd loved so dearly. If not for his work as a firefighter, he might not have emotionally healed. For him, doing a job where it made a difference in terms of life and death had given him a focus again after losing Mika.

"Now that's a sense of civic duty if I ever heard of one," Gabrielle said. She continued to eye him as though she thought there was more to his story, but she didn't ask. He didn't volunteer. Tonight, it was about her.

An audible breath oozed out of her. "My father's heart attack has been so incredibly stressful on my mother, and do you believe that my sister hasn't made it down here to visit him? She gave some excuse about not having a job. What she wants is for my mother to send her money, or me. And I refuse to do it. I talked to her earlier, told her that she better get down here because who knows if our father will make it? I don't care if she has to walk from Portland."

Gabrielle's voice cracked, and Omar moved closer still, slipping and arm around her shoulder. "Hey," he said softly. "It's going to be okay."

"My parents did so much for us, and I'm so angry

that Grace continues to find any justifiable excuse to stay away. If she's not working, she's in the best position to be at our parents' house and help my mother care for my dad. I have a full-time job which is demanding. But I don't want to desert them."

"I'm not going to presume to tell you what you should do. But if your sister truly is having a hard time financially—for whatever reason—maybe this is a time where you could make an exception. When I say that, it's only because I agree that she needs to be here. And I get your stand on principle, but if your dad does die, and she said she couldn't make it here because of lack of funds… That's something that might weigh on you in the future."

She opened her mouth to speak, but Omar held up a hand to silence her. "Trust me, I've seen it. I've seen tragedy at fire scenes, car accidents. I've witnessed people taking a stand because they believed it was right, but ultimately cost them in other ways. Whatever it may cost you to get your sister down here is a small price to pay in terms of knowing you did the right thing. In case the worst happens with your father."

Gabrielle looked down, but nodded. "You sound like my friend Pauline. She tells me all the time that I need to be not quite so hard-nosed. Especially where my sister is concerned. But with her, it's been one disappointment after the other."

"I get it. But you can only control you."

"That something else Pauline would say," Gabrielle said, offering him a little chuckle. "Maybe I should introduce you to her. She's single," she added, her tone flippant.

Omar felt a sinking sensation in his gut. They had been

making headway, getting along well. And now she was going to say something like that?

"I'm not here with you because I want to meet your friend. I'm here with you because… Don't you get it? I'm madly attracted to you. No matter how many times you've pushed me away, I couldn't stay away."

He saw her swallow. "I guess I shouldn't quit my day job. Being a comedian isn't working out so well for me." Her lips curled in a small smile. "Honestly, I appreciate you being here. More than you know. Between my father, and trying to keep my mother strong, and wondering if my sister's going to show up and what happened with my ex-fiancé… There are days when I feel incredibly alone."

"You're not alone." She looked up at him, and he stared into her eyes. He wanted her to know that he meant that.

"I appreciate that."

Then she leaned against him and snuggled, and he put his arms around her.

Omar felt a heady sensation of happiness and emotion. She was turning to him in her time of need, and it was the kind of responsibility that carried a lot of weight. He felt honored to be the one with her right now, and hoped that his presence would help ease her pain.

"I can't even believe you're here with me right now," Gabrielle said. "It's something I never thought would happen."

"Quite frankly, neither did I." He trailed his fingertips down her exposed arm. "Can I ask you a question?"

"Sure."

"If you don't want to talk about it right now, it's okay," he said. "But you made a comment more than once about my reputation preceding me. Far as I know, I don't know anyone you know. So for you to talk about my reputation confuses me."

She didn't answer right away, and Omar figured she was debating whether or not she should. "You used to date someone that I knew," she finally said. "It was a friend of a friend, actually. But I heard all about it. A complicated love triangle… They made you out to be one of the biggest players around."

Omar eased back to look at her. "Who are you talking about?"

"A woman named Irene. And I think the other woman involved in the love triangle was named Kerry, or Sheri. Something like that."

So that's what this was about. "What did you hear?" Omar asked.

"All I know is that Irene thought things were so serious with you and that you might propose. She didn't find out about Kerry until a while later. Things got ugly. This was a few years ago, so I don't know all the details. But…" She sighed softly. "We don't have to talk about this, Omar."

"No, I want to talk about it," Omar said. "You may think that you know something about me, but that doesn't mean you do."

"Really? So you weren't seeing Irene and another woman at the same time? Irene wasn't devastated by your betrayal? I heard all the juicy details from our mutual friend. You left her wrecked."

"I never lied to Irene. We never had a relationship."

Gabrielle scoffed. "Of course not. You just sleep with someone, but it's not a relationship, right? For you, it's just a pastime."

"You are making a lot of assumptions. Do you want to hear my side of the story, or not?"

Gabrielle did something that he didn't expect. She

slipped her arms around his neck and edged her face closer to his. "It doesn't matter. We're both adults. And you're right, I've been pushing you away because… Well, because I was being too emotional about everything. Right now, I want this." Gently, she kissed his lips.

She looked up into his eyes, and he could see the heat pooling in their depths. But this wasn't how he wanted her. "What exactly are you saying? That you don't care if I'm a player?"

"It's been a long time since I've been to bed with anyone," Gabrielle said, her voice husky. "And I'm attracted to you. Isn't that all that matters?"

"Heck no, that's not all that matters."

She shifted her body, easing up so that she could kiss him more easily. She tightened her arms around his neck as her lips moved over his. "It's okay," she whispered against his mouth. "And honestly, I don't want to talk anymore."

She slipped her tongue over his lip, something that would otherwise turn him on. But right now, all he could think about was the reality. She thought he was a player. And worse, she probably thought he was a liar. God only knew why she wanted to share her bed with him.

"Come on, Omar. Kiss me back. Make me forget…"

"So that's what this is about? You need a break from the stress in your life?"

She eased backward and smiled at him. Then she started to unbutton her blouse. "The attraction between us is undeniable. I believe you said something before about ending the torture?"

Words he now regretted. He'd let his lust control his mouth, and it wasn't how he'd wanted to portray himself with Gabrielle. Yes, he wanted to make love to her. There was no doubt about that. But he wasn't interested in sex with no strings attached.

Her blouse undone, she all but threw herself at him and began kissing him again.

"Gabrielle—"

"No, don't talk." She put a finger on his lips to silence him. "It's finally time to act."

Chapter 16

Gabrielle gave him a soft peck. Then another. And then her mouth was parting, and she was flicking her tongue across his bottom lip.

"Whoa, whoa, whoa," Omar said, and tried to ease away from her.

She wouldn't let him. She kept her arms locked around his neck. "I want this," she whispered.

"You didn't want this before—"

"Forget about before. I want this right now."

And then she started kissing him again, and this time her hands were sliding down from around his neck and onto his chest. She was groping him, and it was all a little too urgent. All so unexpected.

Though there was nothing more that Omar wanted than to slip his hands around her waist and pull her against his body, he did the exact opposite. He took her hands in his and pried them off his body.

"Trust me," he began, "there's nothing I want more than to make love to you. But this is all a little too sudden. It feels—"

"Sudden?" Gabrielle asked. Undeterred, her hands went to the top button on his shirt. "Why would it bother you that this is sudden? I'm offering you sex. I know this is what you want. You made that clear from the beginning."

"Why would it bother me that it's sudden?" Omar echoed, looking at her with disbelief. So that's what she thought? That all she had to do was throw herself at him and he wouldn't think, he'd simply act? "Your father had another heart attack. In a few days, he's going to be having a high-risk surgery. You're hurting, Gabrielle. What you're doing right now—it's like what you said, about escaping. What kind of jerk would I be to take advantage of you in the situation?"

"Really? I'm offering you sex and you're worrying about taking advantage of me? This is sex on a platter, Omar. No strings attached. Isn't that what a hot guy like you wants?"

Omar frowned at her. Was this the wine talking, or was she expressing her true feelings? "Your opinion of me is far lower than I ever thought," he said. "You expect me to take sex because it's offered to me on a platter? You think I have no discernment at all?"

She looked up at him, her eyes registering surprise. "Okay, I'm sorry. I shouldn't have said that. The point is, you like me. You told me that. And you made no bones about telling me that you know I'm attracted to you, too. Finally, I'm admitting it. I want you." She gently stroked his face. "I want to make love."

"And this has nothing to do with your father? Hours

ago, you were weeping. Now… You want to go to bed with a guy you've been running from?"

"If I've been running from you, I've been doing a pretty bad job. We both know that." She paused, and her chest heaved and fell with a heavy breath. "I know I'm probably not making much sense, but I guess what I'm saying is that… I need you tonight. Yes, I do need to forget. And if we have tonight… There's no pressure that it has to be anything more than tonight. I'm not going to expect flowers and candles and you don't have to worry that you'll hurt me like you did Irene."

"Okay that's enough." Omar got up from the sofa.

"Sit back down."

"No." He saw the baffled expression on her face.

"No, as in you're turning me down?"

"I'm turning you down," he said, making his position clear. "I don't want sex—not like this. I'm not here to be a machine and take sex just because you're offering it to me. And heck, Gabrielle. Not under these circumstances. Not after some of the things you've said."

She looked up at him, confusion and perhaps hurt stirring in her beautiful eyes. Man, he was attracted to her. But her opinion of him was abysmal.

"Whatever you heard about me," Omar continued, "I'm not what you think. I've been telling you that since the beginning, but it seems you don't believe me. Contrary to whatever you think, and perhaps what others believe, I don't take sex from everyone who offers it to me. I need to be attracted to the person. I happen to be attracted to you, yes. But it's more than just a physical attraction. I thought I made that clear. I have no interest in just getting in your pants. So this whole act right now—as if I'm not even supposed to consider the circumstances, and just jump into bed with you—I find it offensive."

Gabrielle's lips parted, but she said nothing. But in her eyes, Omar could see the mix of conflicted emotions. She hadn't expected him to reject her. Did she really expect him to behave like a guy with no consideration for a woman in pain and just jump into bed with her? What kind of jerk would that make him?

But that was exactly what she had expected. He could see it in her face.

"All right," she said. "We don't have to have sex."

When he started walking toward the front door, she said, "What are you doing?"

"I'm leaving." He started toward the door. "I can get my dishes another time." He simply wanted to get out of here.

"So you're running away from me?" Gabrielle asked. "After all that talk about being attracted to me and kissing me and touching me and…making me want you?"

"Apparently, you think I'm some unfeeling guy who's only motivated by sex." His gut tightened, just knowing that's what she thought about him. He waved a dismissive hand. "I've got to go."

"What?"

He didn't answer as he walked the rest of the way to her front door. The truth was, he would want nothing more than to stay and make love to Gabrielle. But not under these circumstances. Not when she thought so lowly of him.

At the door, he looked over his shoulder at her. She remained sitting on the sofa, looking befuddled. "For what it's worth," he began, "Irene was kind of crazy. Actually, she was downright crazy. I never made her any promises, but she misrepresented our relationship to everyone she spoke to. It would have been nice if you'd asked me my side of the story, instead of assuming that you knew."

"Omar…"

He opened the door and quickly walked out of Gabrielle's house.

Gabrielle flinched when the door shut. Her heart was beating furiously. Omar was actually leaving.

She'd offered him sex, and he turned her down.

A myriad of emotions were swirling around in her. But the overwhelming one was one of rejection.

She got to her feet and ran to her front door. She saw Omar getting into his car.

"Omar, wait!" she called.

For a moment, she thought he was going to get in the car and drive away. But he stopped and turned to look over his shoulder at her.

Gabrielle stepped onto the porch. "Don't go." She exhaled sharply. "You're right. I should have asked you what happened."

But it had been easier for her to believe the negative. Because she was still guarding her heart. And lowering that guard wasn't easy.

"If you think it's only because you didn't ask me about Irene—"

"No, I know. I offended you. What I said… Not sure why I said it." She did know why. It was because she didn't want to make herself seem vulnerable. "I'm sorry. Look, can we forget what I just did? How I behaved?"

"I'm not going to have sex with you, Gabrielle."

She nodded, understanding. And right now, the mood had fizzled. She had treated Omar like an object. Even worse, like a brainless object. "No sex," she said. "I just really don't want to be alone right now."

He looked at her, and she could see the internal conflict on his face. He wanted to go. Heck, he probably never wanted to see her again.

"Maybe the stress of everything is getting to me," she said, and she could hear the vulnerable hitch to her voice. Her chest tightening, she continued. "I'm not really acting like myself." She took another step closer to him. "We can watch a movie. Talk. Just stay with me."

Gabrielle saw the rise and fall of Omar's Adam's apple, then heard a gentle exhalation of his breath. "All right," he said, and closed the door of his SUV.

She smiled. "Thank you," she said when he walked back over to her. "I just… I don't want to be alone tonight."

Omar's eyes narrowed. "You want me to stay the night?"

She nodded. "I have a spare bedroom. It's rarely ever used. This house is always so…empty. I don't want it to be empty tonight. I promise, I'll be on my best behavior."

"I'll stay," Omar told her.

Feeling a sense of relief, Gabrielle walked back into her house. Omar followed her inside.

"I wouldn't mind watching a movie," he said. "And I see you have quite the collection."

"Would you believe I buy them and I pretty much never watch them? Tobias—my ex—always promised to watch some of the scary ones with me, but he never did. And I haven't had anyone else around to watch them with."

"I love scary movies. What do you have?"

Three hours later, the movie was over, and Gabrielle and Omar sat on the sofa, talking.

Gabrielle still felt bad about what she had said to Omar, but at least he didn't seem to be holding a grudge. He was an enigma. Everything she'd heard about him—everything she'd sensed about him—made her believe that he was the type of guy who would appreciate casual sex.

She had made assumptions where he was concerned, and they were all turning out to be untrue.

In her own defense, she wasn't good at initiating casual sex. Maybe she should have just shut up about what she thought he wanted, and concentrated on what she wanted.

Though she doubted Omar would have had sex with her anyway. He'd been acutely aware of the fact that she was running from pain, and he didn't want to take advantage of her. He was honorable.

Which was more than she could say for herself.

Gabrielle glanced at the wall clock. It was nearly twelve-thirty in the morning. "I know I asked you to stay with me the night," she began, then yawned. "But I feel a lot better than I did earlier. I am just going to head to bed, sleep till the morning. So you don't need to be here."

"Do you want me to leave?"

"I am just saying… If you don't want to stay…"

"You said you didn't want to be alone tonight." He shrugged. "And since you're not that good in the kitchen, I could stay in, make you a nice breakfast in the morning. If you want."

A small smile curled at the corners of Gabrielle's mouth. "A home-cooked breakfast? Hash browns, scrambled eggs?"

"If that is what you want…"

"How can I pass up that?"

"We have a deal, then."

She yawned again. "I hope you don't mind that I go to bed now. I'm exhausted."

He stood to meet her. "Just show me where the spare bedroom is."

She took a step, then paused. "About earlier… I just want to apologize again. You're not what I thought at all. I totally misjudged you."

"I accept your apology."

As he offered her his classic sexy grin, Gabrielle felt desire warm her veins. She wanted to kiss him. But not in the crazy manner she had before. She wanted to kiss him slowly—not to forget—but because she wanted to experience a connection with the guy she was truly attracted to.

"Which way?" Omar asked.

"Right." She couldn't attempt kissing him again. Not after what had happened earlier.

She led the way out of the living room and down the hallway, stopping at the first bedroom on the right. She opened it, and gestured to the queen-size bed that was inside. "There you go. That's the bed. As you can see, it's already made up. The linens are clean—I rarely have guests staying over. I do have an extra new toothbrush in the bathroom cabinet."

"Thanks."

She looked up at him, realizing that now, as they stood outside the door, her heart was thumping faster and harder than before. He was about to retire to bed. In her house. Had she really blown it? Or would he invite her to join him?

"You want to know something?" he asked softly.

"What?"

"I really, *really* want to kiss you right now." He tucked a strand of her hair behind her ear. "But I won't."

Her lips parted in invitation. She *did* want him to kiss her.

"Because… If I start to kiss you, I'm not sure I'll be able to stop. And I promised myself that when I agreed to stay, I wouldn't have sex tonight."

"Did I blow it?" The words tumbled from Gabrielle's mouth of their own accord.

He stroked her cheek. "I just believe that some things are worth waiting for."

Chapter 17

Gabrielle awoke with a start. Her eyes greeted the darkness. The next instant, an odd sense came over her.

And then, everything came rushing back. The night before with Omar. Him staying the night.

She sat bolt upright. He was in the other room. In the other bed.

She quickly looked at the clock. It was 4:23 in the morning. She wondered if he was awake, or sleeping soundly.

She lay back down, thinking of the evening before. Thinking of his strong arms wrapped around her as they'd watched that scary movie. For a few hours, she had been granted peace. Peace from the turmoil of her life. From the uncertainty regarding the crazy person who was burning down the city, and the fear that her father was going to die.

Her body tingled. Omar was in the other room, sleeping in that bed...

She'd thrown herself at him in a shameless manner. And he'd rejected her. But would he now?

He was the first man to make her feel alive in several months. And she wanted to make love to him. There was nothing more she wanted than to lose herself in his strong arms.

Suddenly, she was throwing off the covers and creeping out of the bed. Then she pattered across the hardwood floor. It was cool beneath her feet. She opened the door as quietly as she could, wondering if this was a bad idea.

But she didn't want to think anymore. All she wanted to do was feel. Feel alive.

And whenever she was around Omar, she felt incredibly alive.

She walked down the hallway and got to his door. She found it ajar. She pushed it open, and it squeaked slightly. Cringing, she stopped, wondering again if this was a bad idea.

If he was sleeping soundly, she didn't want to wake him up.

No, that wasn't true. She did want to wake him up. He was here, in her home. And she didn't want to miss this opportunity.

Drawing in a deep breath, she started into the room. She knew this was a bold move, especially after what had happened the night before. And yet…

She was going for it.

She walked quietly into the room. Reaching the bed, she could see that he was confined to one side. He was facing her, and the streetlight from outside illuminated the room enough for her to see that his eyes were closed. He was sleeping. Should she even do this?

She was like a woman in heat, and once again she felt

ashamed of herself. She'd kept him up late; he was sleeping peacefully. This was a bad idea.

She turned on her heel and started to retreat.

"Hey."

The deep sound of his voice made her stop in her path. Her pulse picked up speed. She turned around, saying sheepishly, "Sorry."

"For what?"

"For waking you up."

"I wasn't sleeping," Omar said.

She wanted to ask if it was for the same reason that she wasn't sleeping well tonight. Just knowing that he was in the other room made it hard for her to get any rest. Every time she closed her eyes, she thought about him. About doing with him what two adults who were attracted to each other would naturally do.

She swallowed. Then she started toward the bed. She sat on the edge and looked down at him. He was naked from the waist up, the sheets strewn over his hips. Seeing him like this, she wanted him even more.

"I haven't been able to sleep much either," she said softly.

"Why not?" Omar asked.

He had to know. Didn't he? "Because it was hard sleeping knowing you were in the other room. Knowing that all I wanted to do was be in bed with you."

Had she really just said that?

She saw Omar's lips form a smile. And then her heart began to pound. He reached his hand out and put it on her arm, then began gently stroking his fingers against her skin. "And I haven't been able to sleep knowing that you were in the other room."

Her womb tightened. The words made her feel heady

and completely desired. She didn't remember ever feeling this kind of magnetic intense attraction.

"I know what you said last night," she began. "But I'm not here right now because of grief. I'm here because I want you. I want to make love."

His hand went up to her shoulder, then he eased up on an elbow so that he could frame her face. "And what I said last night… It doesn't actually apply anymore."

She looked at him through narrowed eyes. "What do you mean? I don't remember what you're talking about."

"Last night, I told you that when I agreed to stay, I thought I wouldn't have sex *that night*. But it's a new day now."

Her heart spasmed in her chest. Her breathing became ragged.

"Come here," Omar rasped. Guiding her face to his, he began to kiss her. And that first touch of his lips on hers, dear God. Heat filled her instantly, desire pooling inside her, hot and sweet. His tongue delved into her mouth, and she placed a hand on his chest. His warm, naked chest. She could feel his beating heart. It matched the frantic beat of her own.

"Omar…" she purred.

He pulled the covers aside so that she could climb under with him. It was warm. Her naked legs skimmed his, and she looped her arm around his neck. He pulled her closer, and she stretched out her body alongside his. She opened her mouth wide, giving him more access to her as he hungrily kissed her. She wanted to give him every bit of her.

His hand moved from her face and smoothed down the front of her body, over her breast and then down to the hem of her short silk nightie. He slipped his fingers underneath the garment and onto her thigh. His hand was cool against her skin, and yet his touch was scorching.

"Do you know how beautiful you are?" Omar asked as his hand crept up her thigh.

"*You* make me feel beautiful," she whispered.

He groaned as his lips captured hers again. His hand smoothed over her hip, moving in slow circles.

Gabrielle shifted her body so that she was lying on her back. Omar's hand moved with her, and now rested on her stomach. The kiss changed from being hot and hungry to slow and deep and sensual.

He moved his mouth from her lips to her neck, his lips creating a path of heat along her skin. Gabrielle gripped his shoulders, the sensations flooding her body making her delirious.

Easing back, Omar looked into her eyes. Gabrielle boldly met his gaze, letting him know that she wanted this.

"Kiss me," she begged.

He brought his lips down on hers. It was soft and oh so sweet. His lips moved slowly, heightening the sexual tension between them. Gabrielle arched her back, urging him to touch her.

Omar's hand moved from her belly, going lower. He bypassed her most feminine spot, and put a hand on her leg just below the juncture of her thighs. Gabrielle exhaled sharply, anticipating his sweet touch.

But he didn't touch her. Not there, anyway. His fingers created a dance of heat and sensation along her inner thigh. Groaning, he deepened the kiss.

She was heady from the desire, from the thrill of his lips on hers. And when—finally—his hand slipped beneath her panties and he stroked her, the pleasure was intense. "Oh, yes…"

"My goodness," Omar said softly. "You're ready for me."

She angled a leg over his body and ran her toes against his thigh. "I've never wanted anything more," she whispered.

His hands deftly encircled her body and pulled her close. Her mouth reached for his, and the kiss was explosive. He suckled her tongue, gripped her hips, his breathing ragged.

With a moan, Gabrielle quickly moved so that she was on top of Omar, her legs straddled over his body. Even in the darkness, she saw how his eyes widened. She pulled her nightie up over her hips, quickly giving him enough access. Then decided that no, this wouldn't do. She pulled the nightie over her head and tossed it onto the floor.

But Omar didn't look at her nakedness... Not yet. He held her gaze, making her feel their connection was so much more intimate. Then, he lowered his eyes to look at breasts.

"Wow." He stared at her in wonder, simply taking in the sight of her without touching her. "Your body is amazing."

He made her feel beautiful. He made her feel as though this connection between them was something that he couldn't possibly share with anyone else.

He raised his hand to her breast, and used his fingers to delicately trace the mounds of her flesh. He was drawing out her pleasure—and her agony. Because she wanted him to touch her where she would feel the most sensation. But he touched everywhere else instead.

When he reached for her hand, she didn't expect it. He linked fingers with hers, and only then did he touch her nipple with his other hand. He touched as though he were a man exploring a woman's breasts for the first time.

Gently. With a sense of awe and reverence. He slowly traced her areola, and her nipple hardened at his touch.

Gabrielle mewled.

Omar took her nipple between two of his fingers and he tweaked and tugged on it. "Omar..."

"I can't believe how beautiful you are."

Did he say this to everyone? Because in her heart, she didn't believe that. She didn't think this was simply bedroom talk. She felt a connection between them, something true and real. She'd felt it from the beginning.

His hand moved up from her breast and snaked around the back of her neck. He urged her down. Then he was kissing her, his tongue deftly sweeping across her mouth in broad strokes, intensifying her desire.

He took her breast in his hand and guided it to his mouth. And oh, the feeling of his tongue on her nipple. He sucked slowly, his tongue twirling around her areola. As Gabrielle began to moan louder, he grazed her nipple with his teeth.

"Oh, my goodness..."

Then he was drawing her nipple into his mouth, and suckling like a starved man. The sensations were exquisite. She moved her body against his, feeling his impressive erection beneath her where she was straddled over him. She wanted so badly for him to be inside her.

But Omar had other plans. Suddenly, he was moving her onto her back. His mouth went to her other nipple, and he teased it into an erect state. He flicked his tongue across the taut peak over and over again. And as he did, he slipped his hand beneath her panties and found her center of pleasure.

His mouth on her breast, his fingers on her center... Oh, the pleasure... The delicious vibrations...

The fierce need.

She arched her back and tightened her legs around his hand. She was lost. Lost in a sea of sensations.

His mouth found hers again, and he kissed her slowly as his fingers worked their magic. Kissed her as her passionate rasps became quicker. Kissed her as she experienced sweet release.

She was panting, her body on sensory overload. Omar continued to kiss her as she rode the glorious wave of bliss.

Only when her breathing slowed did he break the kiss and ease backward. He made quick work of taking off his boxers and tossing them onto the floor. He opened his bedside drawer, withdrew a condom, and put it on. Then, he moved back over to her, and she moved her underwear down over her hips. He kissed her leg as he pulled the pantie completely off her body.

Lying beside her on the bed, he gently fingered her nipple before taking it into his mouth again. Her body exploded with fresh heat. Gabrielle dug her fingers into his back and moaned at the onslaught of pleasure.

Omar's hand traveled down over her abdomen, and then lower to between her thighs. He guided her legs apart.

He was stroking her again, causing heat to build in her like an inferno. Then, a groan rumbling in his chest, he eased his body on top of hers.

Feeling his impressive shaft against her, she could hardly breathe.

"I like you," he said softly. "A lot."

Emotion filled her. She could already feel herself falling for him. He was gorgeous, and he was kind. And the chemistry between them was off the charts.

"I like you, too," she whispered.

"Baby..." he rasped.

Then he guided himself into her. And oh, that first moment when he filled her was utterly sweet. It was as if she was experiencing this delectable sensation for the first time.

He moved slowly, and filled her deeply. Gabrielle's moan was long and loud. She wrapped her legs around him and gripped his back. She didn't want to let him go.

"You okay?" he asked.

Gabrielle stroked his face. "Yes, baby."

Omar eased back, then thrust deep. He did it again, and again. Gabrielle gyrated her body against his, letting him know that she was more than okay. He didn't have to treat her like a delicate flower.

He thrust deep into her, and her lips parted on a rapturous moan. Then he was kissing her. Kissing her and tangling his tongue with hers as their bodies united as one. Gabrielle urged her hips upward to meet each thrust, and their pace slowly began to quicken.

Nothing had felt so good. Nothing. The world right now consisted of only her and Omar, and she never wanted to leave this special place.

"Omar... Oh, my goodness... I feel so..." Her words seemed to spur him on, because he picked up the pace. His strokes were deeper, longer and reaching her in a place she didn't expect to be touched.

Her heart.

She pressed her lips into his shoulder as they continued to ride the wave of pleasure together.

Had she ever been this alive?

Dexterously, Omar moved their bodies so that suddenly she was on top of him. They were still joined intimately, and Gabrielle felt a whole new onslaught of sensations being in this position. She looked down at him, her eyes connecting with his as their bodies moved together faster and faster.

The sensation was building. She felt it spiraling through her whole body. And suddenly, she was flying over the edge into the sweetest abyss. She arched her back, and rode the wave. Omar covered her breasts and moved even faster.

Omar's breathing was labored now, his strokes quick and rhythmic. His hands went to her hips and he helped them down as he continued to love her. Then, he grunted and dug his fingers into her skin as his own release came.

Gabrielle looked down at Omar, at his parted lips, at the expression in his eyes as he came undone. He stared right back, allowing her to see him at his most vulnerable moment.

She dropped her body down onto his, and he tightened his arms around her and held her close. The two of them stayed in the same position for a long while, their slick bodies against one another's, their ragged breathing filling the bedroom.

And something filled Gabrielle's heart…

Something she didn't expect.

Something she wasn't sure she was prepared for.

Chapter 18

Was it written on her face that Gabrielle had just had the best sex of her life?

Because as she strode into the cable TV station, she thought she saw eyes widen with curiosity when her co-workers looked in her direction.

"Morning," Janine said, giving her an odd look.

"Good morning," Gabrielle replied, and realized that she sounded a little too perky.

Oh, well. She *was* perky. Nothing wrong with that.

When she neared the reception desk, Renée's eyes brightened—then narrowed with question.

"Good morning, Renée," Gabrielle greeted her.

"Good morning," Renée echoed. But she said the words almost like a question.

Was Gabrielle somehow broadcasting to the world that she'd gotten laid last night?

She didn't break stride as she headed into her office,

and no sooner than she was rounding her desk, Renée was at her office door. Her eyes danced as she looked at her.

"What is it?" Gabrielle asked.

"Your shirt…"

"My shir—" Gabrielle began to ask, at first not understanding. But then it hit her. She quickly glanced down, and saw that remaining portion of the tag she'd cut out—the thin white strip still evident in the shirt's seam—was showing. Not only had Gabrielle put her shirt on inside out, she'd also put it on backward.

No wonder everyone had been giving her an odd look! How had she not noticed this before?

Goodness, what everyone must be thinking! And yet, Gabrielle almost smiled.

She hadn't gotten nearly enough sleep to be coherent this morning, because she'd had a man rocking her world last night.

Gabrielle wanted to do a happy dance.

"Oh, wow," Gabrielle said to Renée. "Not sure where my mind is. Renée, would you mind getting me a coffee? I clearly need it."

Renée continued to look at her with a sense of fascination, but nodded. "Sure thing."

When Renée disappeared, Gabrielle closed her door and quickly took off her top and put it on the right way. Good grief, how embarrassing!

She started laughing. How nice it was to have a little chaos in her structured life. Good chaos, that is. To be lost in something so wonderful that she'd actually put her clothes on the wrong way. She felt alive for the first time in a long time.

When the knock sounded on the door, Gabrielle called, "Come in."

"Here's your coffee," Renée said. She crossed the room

and brought it to her desk in her favorite mug. Then, clearly unable to hide her curiosity, Renée said, "The suspense is killing me. It's not like you to come in here looking anything than less-than-perfect. What's going on?"

"Why do you think something's going on?" Gabrielle asked, trying to keep a straight face.

"I don't know. I'm thinking it could have something to do with a certain firefighter…"

Gabrielle's heart thumped. How did Renée know?

"Why would you say that?"

"You slept with him, didn't you!" Renée's eyes filled with excitement.

"Renée, I have to work." Gabrielle's tone wasn't near as stern as she'd tried to pull off. In fact, there was a hint of amusement in her voice.

Renée went to the door, closed it, then faced Danielle and squealed. "I can't believe you hooked up with Omar!"

"I didn't say I did."

"But you didn't say you didn't," Renée countered. "You have to tell me! I'm dying here."

"I may have been…busy last night… So busy that I was not quite myself when I got dressed this morning."

Renée did a little dance on the spot, and Gabrielle had to wonder why news of her having a love life could cause such a reaction. Had she really been sulking, as Pauline had told her?

"How did you know?" Gabrielle asked.

"Girl, if he came around here any more, I was going to give him an application for a job." Renée beamed. "It was obvious he was into you, and you definitely had the hots for him."

"It was obvious?"

"Maybe not to everyone else. But I saw this happening." Renée lifted her hand. Gabrielle high-fived her.

Gabrielle's office line rang. "All right, Renée. I've got to get to work. Mum's the word, okay?"

Renée mimed zipping her lips shut.

Gabrielle saw the last guest out of the studio once the taping of *Your Hour* was finished. "Thank you so much for coming in today. I loved hearing about your soccer academy for underprivileged children. It's so nice that you give back."

Her eyes caught the reception desk—and the large bouquet of red roses that was there. Her heart pounded.

The coach shook her hand. "Thanks for havin' me."

"Take care. And let us know about any new developments in the future. You're welcome back on the show anytime."

Once the man was heading to the exit, Gabrielle rushed over to the reception desk. Renée was already beaming at her. And she knew.

"Girl, this delivery came while you were in the studio."

"For me?"

"I'd love to say they're for me," Renée said. "But no. These are definitely for you."

Gabrielle quickly snatched up the card inserted into the roses. My goodness, there were more than a dozen. Maybe two. And they were gorgeous. Mixed with baby's breath, the bouquet was dazzling.

She opened the card.

Wow
Xoxo Omar

Gabrielle's face flamed as she grinned from ear to ear. "From Omar?" Renée asked.

"Yeah."

Renée smiled.

Gabrielle took the vase with the roses and carried them to her office. She was touched. She was giddy. She hadn't expected this.

Once behind her desk, she called Omar. "Hey, beautiful," he answered.

She felt a rush of giddiness all over again. "I got the roses. And the card," she added with a giggle. "They're beautiful."

"Not as beautiful as you."

"I want to see you again," Gabrielle said.

"Me, too."

"Tonight's no good. I have to go to the hospital tonight."

"And I work tomorrow," Omar told her.

"You did promise me a home-cooked breakfast."

"Yeah, well I would have been able to make it this morning… If someone wasn't so insatiable last night."

Gabrielle giggled again. She literally felt like a schoolgirl. She was on cloud nine. She was bubbly and excited. She hadn't felt like this in…in forever.

"We're going to have to touch base to see what works," Gabrielle said. "My dad's surgery is on Friday, so I don't know."

"Let me know if you need me there."

"On Friday?"

"Sure," Omar said. "I can be there for you."

Again, she was touched. He was being so sweet.

"By the way," she said. "I took your advice."

"Oh?"

"I called my sister this morning and as expected, she said she didn't have the money for the flight. So I'm buying her ticket. You're absolutely right. She needs to be here for our dad, and if I can make it happen…then I should."

"Wow," Omar commented. "You're softening on me."

"Must be something about you," Gabrielle said.

She suddenly wondered if she was gushing too much. But she wanted to spend more time with him, and wasn't ashamed to say it.

Yet she knew she needed to take things in stride and not get too ahead of herself.

"I'll talk to you later, okay?" she said.

"You bet."

"So, was it fast and furious?" Pauline asked Gabrielle later at their favorite restaurant. Before heading to the hospital, Gabrielle decided to meet up with Pauline to share the news about what had happened with Omar. "I need to know all the details."

"Pauline!"

"What? You expected me not to ask after how you gushed on the phone?"

Gabrielle blushed. She had gushed, hadn't she? She just felt so amazing that she wanted to shout it from the mountaintop. Of course, she couldn't do that. The next best thing was confiding in her best friend.

"You have to tell me, girl. Because I take credit for the fact that you're no longer sulking. No longer walking around like there's a dark cloud hanging over your head. If I didn't give you that encouragement to get your groove on…"

Gabrielle leaned forward on the table and spoke in a hushed tone. "Well, if you must know. It *was* fast and furious… One of the times. Another time it was hot and slow. And another time—"

"Okay, you are killing me! Multiple times and you somehow managed to make it to work this morning?"

"Barely. And get this. My shirt was on inside out *and* backward. Girl, I was a hot mess." Gabrielle smirked. "Yet I couldn't stop smiling."

Pauline reached across the table and high-fived her. "That's what I'm talking about."

"I feel like a whole new person. And now I get exactly what you were talking about. Tobias... Who the heck is Tobias?" She laughed.

"See, now you have it out of your system. You got a good—whatever you want to call it—last night, and now you can move on. You never have to see him again, and yet you feel so much better, don't you?"

Gabrielle's smile faltered somewhat. The idea of not seeing him again was one she didn't want to contemplate. But she didn't want to admit that to Pauline, who was clearly in favor of having a fling and moving on.

"That's the beauty of the booty call," Pauline was saying when Gabrielle tuned in again.

"Yeah," Gabrielle said. "I guess it is."

Pauline was about to put a tortilla chip into her mouth, but halted. She leveled a curious gaze on Gabrielle. "Wait a second. This *was* a booty call, wasn't it? You didn't catch feelings for him?"

"No." Gabrielle reached for a chip, not facing her friend. "Of course not. Like you said, I feel great... Better than I ever have, actually."

Pauline leaned forward, staring at her with wide eyes. "Oh, my goodness," she said in a low tone. "You *did* catch feelings."

"Why would you say that?"

"I can see it in your expression. Hear it in your voice."

Gabrielle didn't say anything for a moment. When

she spoke, her words were calculated. "I'm just thinking that maybe it doesn't have to be a onetime thing? It was great last night. I mean, truly phenomenal. I wouldn't mind more of that."

"Really?" Pauline eased back in her seat, a look of curiosity playing in her eyes. "After the way you spoke about this guy?"

"Yet you encouraged me not to worry about his character and get busy, anyway."

"Yeah, because he sounded like perfect booty call material." Pauline shrugged. "I suppose a booty call doesn't have to be a onetime thing. You can have him on speed dial, I guess. It's just... I know you. I think the more you spend time with him, the more likely you might start to feel something for him. And given what you said about him, I would hate to see you fall for the wrong guy."

"I may have misjudged him," Gabrielle admitted.

"Whoa." Pauline's eyebrows shot up. "What does that mean?"

Gabrielle shrugged while nibbling on a chip. "Nothing really. I'm just... I guess I'm just saying that he's not exactly who I thought he was. I saw him as being this guy who would just have sex and move on."

"You don't think he's moving on?"

Gabrielle thought of how to answer the question. "He said he wants to see me again."

"Okay..."

"Overall, he's not the jerk I thought he was. He took me to the hospital the other night when my dad had a second heart attack. He offered to be there with me on Friday when my dad has his triple bypass."

"You like him."

"As a person, yeah. As a lover... For sure. Look, you know I'm not a casual sex kind of girl. So I thought I would feel… I don't know—maybe ashamed to some extent the morning after? Maybe have some regret? But I don't. I think that for what it was worth, it meant something. And that's nice."

Pauline was looking at her with a curious expression.

"What?" Gabrielle asked.

"It's already happening."

"What is?" Gabrielle asked.

"I can see it in your eyes. You're already falling for him."

Gabrielle scoffed. "No. I'm not."

"Yes. I totally see it." Pauline shook her head, though there was a small smile playing on her lips. "Girl, don't you know how to just have fun without strings?"

"Sorry I'm not an expert like you!" Gabrielle said, then laughed.

"I'm not an expert, either. I've done it a couple times, and… I guess it was either what I needed or I knew that nothing would come of it. It worked for me. That's why I suggested if for you. But it looks like something else is blooming between you and Omar."

Gabrielle sipped her margarita. "For now, I'm just thinking about how great it was to let loose and get my groove on." She grinned. "I feel like a weight has been lifted from my shoulders. I even called Grace this morning and told her I'd book her a plane ticket so she can come home and be here for our dad."

Pauline's eyes bulged. "Wow. That's huge."

"I just feel better," Gabrielle said. "About everything."

And if that was how she felt after one night with Omar, she wondered how she would feel if she spent even more time with him.

Chapter 19

Gabrielle felt amazing.

The next few weeks were the best of her life. Her father recovered amazingly after his surgery, and Grace was staying at her parents' place to help out. Things were a bit awkward, but Gabrielle was working at rebuilding her relationship with her sister, and from what she could tell, Grace seemed to have had a change of character. Seeing their father in such a weak state had been a wake-up call for her to realize that he truly could possibly die.

Even the arsonist hadn't struck over the past few weeks. All seemed right in the world again.

Omar had been phenomenal. Gabrielle had seen him as much as possible. She couldn't deny that her favorite thing to do was get naked with him.

Their sex was just so hot.

She had gone home after work to change into something special she'd bought just for him. Then she called to make sure that nothing had changed their plans.

"Hey," she said huskily into the phone. "We're still on, right?"

"I'm here. Making you a dinner I think you'll love."

"I can't wait," Gabrielle told him.

He lived about ten minutes away from her, higher in the hills. His home had a spectacular view of the bay. She especially loved his deck. It was a large glass-and-metal structure right on the edge of the hillside. He had a hot tub outside as well as an outdoor dining table and lounge chairs. There were large trees on either side of the deck, which gave it total privacy.

What would it be like to make love outside under the stars? Gabrielle wondered.

She parked in Omar's concrete driveway, then stepped out of her vehicle. Swallowing, she glanced around. Given how she was dressed, she wondered if anyone would give her a second look.

But why should they? It was January in Ocean City. Wearing an overcoat wasn't an odd sight, not with the chill in the air today.

Her four-inch red pumps clinked on the driveway as she made her way to his door. Once there, she checked out her reflection through the glass. Her hair was styled to give it volume, her makeup done to accentuate her eyes and lips.

She felt nervous, anxious to see how Omar would react.

She rang the doorbell.

Thirty seconds later, he was opening the door with a smile. But the next instant, the smile disappeared as his eyes roamed over her from head to toe.

He pushed open the glass door, saying, "Wow."

"Hi," Gabrielle said, her voice soft and fluttery.

"What are you wearing under that?" he asked, and put a finger on the lapel of her overcoat.

"What do you think I'm wearing under it?" she asked.

"I know what I *hope* you're not wearing under there…"

Slipping an arm around her, he pulled her into the house and closed the door. Then he brought his mouth down on hers—hard.

Omar's tongue slipped into Gabrielle's warm, sweet mouth while his hands roamed over her coat from her shoulders down to her butt. He groaned as he pulled her body against his. She was stunning.

And right now, she was every man's fantasy. The short red coat. The red pumps.

Breaking the kiss, he stepped backward. She looked up at him from heavy-lidded eyes. Slowly, he pulled on the tie on her coat until it was undone. Then he slipped open the folds and opened her coat so he could see what she was wearing underneath.

Instantly, his groin pulled with intense desire. She was a vision in red. A satin corset hugged her torso, highlighting her small waist and full hips. And the way her breasts looked pushed up in this garment… Omar swallowed.

He eased the coat off her shoulders. The lacy panty she wore was also red and had little black bows at the sides. There were also black bows at the top of the corset, between her bountiful bosoms, and on the bottom right over where her belly button was.

His lust intensified. Gabrielle was so incredibly beautiful, and dressed like this, she was a vision.

"You like?" she asked, and did a slow twirl.

His entire body filled with heat. She was wearing a thong, exposing her perfect backside.

"Come here," Omar growled, and pulled her body against his. Her soft breasts flattened against his chest, and she purred in response. Looping her arms around his neck, she eased up on her toes and slowly leaned in for another kiss.

She was so soft and sweet and utterly irresistible. She tightened her arms around his neck as the kiss deepened. Her lips parted, and she hungrily flicked her tongue over his.

Omar smoothed his hands down her back. His fingers searched for a way to get this garment off her. It was gorgeous, but it had to go.

"How do you get this thing off?" he muttered.

"Side zipper," Gabrielle whispered. "Easy access."

He grinned down at her, then scooped her into his arms. She made a slight mewling sound as he did, which stoked his inner fires even more.

"Wait," she said. "Weren't you cooking?"

"Don't you worry," he told her. "The only thing cooking will be in the bedroom."

"Mmm." She nibbled on his earlobe. "I like the sound of that."

Ever since letting her guard down, she had become a completely different woman. She was insatiable in the bedroom, and Omar loved it. She seemed unable to get enough of him, and he couldn't get enough of her.

He carried her toward his bedroom, and Gabrielle started kissing the skin on his collarbone. A soft kiss there, a flick of her tongue there.

A ragged breath escaped his lips. Omar wanted to make sweet love to her all night long. He wanted to do it slowly. He wanted to do it fast. He wanted to experience everything with Gabrielle.

Once at the bed, Omar eased Gabrielle down. He gave her a soft kiss before searching for the zipper at her side. But as he looked at her, at how incredible she looked in this sexy red outfit she'd put on just for him, he decided to leave it on.

"You look too hot in this," he whispered. "I'm gonna leave it on."

"Mmm." Gabrielle leaned forward and planted a soft kiss on his chest. He sucked in a breath. Then she dragged her nails down his chest and rubbed her knee along the outside of his leg.

Omar trailed his fingers down her arm. "You really are ravenous, aren't you?"

"Only for you," she said.

Omar slipped his hand beneath the edge of her thong and slowly pulled it over her hips, then dragged it down her legs. He lowered himself onto his haunches, and one foot to take off the thong, then the other.

He smoothed his hands up her smooth legs, and kissed his way up her thigh. And when he reached the center of her femininity, he planted a soft kiss there. When she expelled a soft moan, he kissed her again, then used his tongue to please her until she was panting.

"Oh, baby..." she moaned.

Gently, he urged her onto the bed. Standing tall, he looked down at her. At the way her bosom looked absolutely delectable in that corset. At her naked hips. At those shoes.

And he knew he needed to make love to her slowly. To savor every single moment with gentle, luscious movements.

Omar eased down over her, and she lay back. He held his torso up with his arms. She reached up, her mouth meeting his. And as their lips connected, heat exploded between them. Gabrielle parted her lips, and he kissed her deeply. Hungrily. Only their mouths were touching, not their bodies.

Delirious with lust, Omar slipped a hand into her hair and curled his fingers around her scalp. He was lost in her. Right now, she was the only thing in the world that mattered.

She threw her arms around his neck, and urged him down onto the bed on top of her. She wrapped her thighs around his hips, pressing her naked center against his erection through his sweatpants.

He could no longer stand this sweet torture. "Hold on, sweetheart," Omar said. "I need to get a condom."

Easing off her, Omar went to the night table and got a condom. He put it on as quickly as he could, then returned to Gabrielle. She snaked an arm around his neck and he settled between her thighs. She gyrated against him, which was all the invitation he needed. He guided his shaft into her sweet body and thrust deep.

Crying out, Gabrielle looked up at him. The expression in those bright, beautiful eyes said that she was his.

He eased back, thrust deep. Then did it again. Her lips parted, and soft moans escaped. All the while, she kept her gaze connected to his.

They moved together slowly, the intensity between them building with every stroke. And when Omar heard Gabrielle's breathing start to come in quicker gasps, and felt her body grow tenser, he knew she was right on the edge.

And so was he.

With one deep thrust he buried himself inside her. And together, they went to that magical place of bliss.

Chapter 20

"Did you hear the news?" Janine asked Gabrielle the next day when she got to work.

"No," Gabrielle replied. "What happened?"

"There was another restaurant fire last night. The manager was inside with another worker. Both of them were trapped."

"They died?" Gabrielle asked, her stomach lurching.

"They're in the hospital," Janine said. "Both suffered burns and smoke inhalation as they tried to escape from the building. They're at Ocean City General."

"Oh, my goodness," Gabrielle said. Had the arsonist been in the crowd last night watching the aftermath of his carnage? If Gabrielle had been at the scene of the fire, would she have recognized the arsonist?

Of course, she wouldn't have been there, anyway. She'd been in Omar's arms, making sweet love.

"In light of this new development, I've made a last-minute adjustment to the show's schedule today. Two of the arsonist's other victims are coming in to speak. We're running the pictures you got once again. They're not great, but it can't hurt."

"Okay," Gabrielle said.

"Let me get you the notes on the guests."

"I'll be in my office," Gabrielle said.

When she got to her office, she texted Omar.

Another arson. Two people injured.

Thankfully not killed! TTYL.

The entire show was dedicated to finding the arsonist, and the pictures Gabrielle had taken, along with the description she remembered of the arsonist, were highlighted throughout *Your Hour*. Gabrielle felt especially drained. The fact that two more people had been hurt had brought up the feelings of anxiety and sadness she'd felt over her own parents' restaurant burning down, and the devastation when her father had had a heart attack.

She called her parents as soon as the show was over. Grace answered.

"Hey, Grace," Gabrielle said when her sister answered the phone. "Did you guys hear the news?"

"Yeah. And we just watched the show."

"How's Daddy?"

"Actually, he's doing okay."

"This news hasn't stressed him out?" Gabrielle asked. That was her fear. That the news of another arson would cause her father more stress.

"Mom's keeping his mind off things. They've been like two lovebirds, snuggling in bed and watching movies. Mom says they're making up for all those movie dates they missed over the years."

"Really?" Gabrielle asked. "Huh."

"It's pretty great to see."

"I'm glad," Gabrielle said. It seemed her father had finally turned the corner emotionally. He wasn't concentrating on what he'd lost, but what he had.

Grace, too, had changed. Her mother had told Gabrielle that she was getting up early, helping to cook healthy meals and take care of their dad. Gabrielle couldn't have been more pleased.

"All right," Gabrielle said. "I'll see you guys later."

Gabrielle's first thought after leaving the station was to stop and get an espresso. The day had been long, and she hadn't eaten well. She thought about Pauline's words, and Omar's. She knew she needed to eat a better diet, so instead of stopping for more coffee, she went to a smoothie bar and ordered a power drink filled with hemp and coconut and cacao and spinach. The combination of ingredients wasn't all that appealing, but it promised to keep you alert and fill you up.

And surprisingly, it tasted good.

She got back into her car and started to drive. She was going to head home, change, then go to her parents' for dinner.

It was a routine drive—until she noticed the black car driving behind her. She'd just made a series of turns, and it had followed her every move.

Was it following her? Or was Gabrielle being paranoid?

Suddenly unsure, Gabrielle made a left turn at the next light, when she should have made a right turn. Her eyes were locked on the car two cars behind her. Her action had been quick, out of the blue. Yet she noticed that the black car also quickly got into the left lane, preparing to turn.

"What the heck?" Gabrielle muttered.

It had to be coincidence. There were lots of times two cars traveled on identical paths. It didn't mean that one person was following the other.

She made another left turn. Again, the car followed her.

Gabrielle sped up and got over to the right lane. She turned to the right. This turn would make no sense—given where she had just come from. But lo and behold, the black car did the same.

"Oh, my goodness," Gabrielle uttered. Her heart was beating faster now, fear coursing through her veins. What was this?

The Ocean City Police Department was just up ahead. Gabrielle hit the gas. When she got to the police station, she quickly turned into the parking lot, her car bouncing as she did. Through the rearview mirror, she saw the black car keep going.

Gripping the steering wheel, Gabrielle let out a relieved sob. Then, she pulled the car into an available parking spot and stopped.

She quickly pressed Omar's number into the keypad in her car's console. He picked up after two rings.

"Hey, Gabby," he greeted her.

"Omar," she gasped.

"What?" he asked, sounding alarmed. "What happened?"

"I think… I think I was just followed."

"What do you mean, followed? In your car?"

"I was driving from the station. Suddenly, I saw this black car. Everywhere I turned, it turned. I mean, I don't know if I'm being paranoid—"

"Where are you now?"

"I drove into the parking lot of the police station."

"The one on State Street?" Omar asked.

"Yes."

"Good. I'll be there in ten minutes."

Omar pulled into the parking lot beside Gabrielle's car, and rushed out. His heart was pumping with fear.

As far as he was concerned, he knew exactly why she'd been followed—and who was behind it.

The arsonist.

Omar had seen the show today, the way they had gone after the arsonist hard. Weeks ago, Omar had told her that it had been foolish to so publicly go after the arsonist. That there could be a risk.

He opened the driver's side door of Gabrielle's vehicle, saw her sitting there with a look of fear in her eyes. One that hit him in the gut—hard.

"Come here," he said.

Whimpering, she stepped out of the car and into his arms.

"Damn it, Gabby," he said, easing back to look at her. "I told you that going after the arsonist was dangerous. You've used your show as a platform, and put yourself at risk."

"Maybe I was imagining it," she said, but her words didn't hold conviction.

"We're going into the station," Omar said. "I've already called a friend of mine, a detective. You need to report this."

"I don't think that's necessary," Gabrielle said.

"It *is* necessary," Omar said. "This isn't up for debate."

Gabrielle's eyes narrowed as she looked at him. "I can see you're worried, Omar. But I wasn't hurt."

"But you could have been. This isn't a joke, Gabrielle. I wish you'd just listened to me."

Gabrielle got back into her car.

"What are you doing?" Omar asked. "I told you, we have an appointment for you to report this."

"Will you come in the car and talk to me for a second?" she asked.

Exhaling a frustrated breath, Omar walked to the other side of the vehicle and got in beside Gabrielle. "If you're going to tell me that you don't want to go in—"

"What I want is for you to talk to me. You can't just show up and tell me what I *have* to do."

"Maybe you can't see the bigger picture," Omar said, "but I can."

"So I'm inept?"

"Maybe with regard to people like the arsonist," Omar answered.

Gabrielle's eyes widened with surprise—then indignation. "I see I shouldn't have called you."

When she started to put her key in the ignition, Omar couldn't believe it. "So you're going to spite me by not reporting this?"

"I'm a grown woman. I expect to be respected, not ordered around. I don't know what's gotten into you."

For a moment, Omar said nothing. Gabrielle stared at him, clearly waiting on him to speak.

Omar cleared his throat. "There was another woman who should have listened to me and didn't. And because she didn't, she died."

Gabrielle's eyes widened in surprise.

"If only Mika had listened to me," Omar said, more to himself. It still haunted him. Mika's defiance in the face of danger.

"What?" Gabrielle asked softly.

Omar took a deep breath and faced her. "Years ago, I fell in love with this girl. I was crazy about her. When I met her, I didn't know that she was involved with someone else. She was already planning to leave him, and when she fell for me, she did. It didn't take long for the threats to start. Letters, phone calls. That's when I learned that she had been in an abusive relationship." Omar paused. "It was scary stuff. He wanted her back. Sometimes, he'd follow her in his car. I told Mika that maybe we should cool our relationship down, wait for a while so we didn't tick her ex off. Some of the letters mentioned her new boyfriend…me. But she was having none of it. The way she saw it, he didn't have the right to tell her what to do or how to live her life. Which, in theory, is absolutely right. But when you're dealing with someone crazy…"

"That's why you're so worried about me," Gabrielle said softly. Omar nodded. Then he looked into Gabrielle's eyes, a look of panic upon them. "Oh, my God. Something awful happened."

Even now, fifteen years later, the memory of how Mika had died still hurt him. "He set her apartment on fire while she slept. She didn't have a chance."

"Omar… I'm so sorry."

"It still hurts. I don't know how much she knew. I don't know if she slept through the fire, if the carbon monoxide got to her. Or she got up and was screaming for help and no one could save her." Omar swallowed. "She had smoke inhalation, so she obviously breathed it in. But her body was also badly burned. I just… I pray she never went through the pain of burning alive."

"Oh, Omar." Gabrielle stroked his face. "That's horrible. And what you must have gone through…"

"They caught the guy, thankfully. He's serving a life sentence. But I still wish I had done something differently. That I had been there for Mika that night. Maybe I should have just broken up with her as a way to lessen her ex's anger…"

"No," Gabrielle said softly. "Don't do that to yourself."

"But the way she died…"

"Omar, don't do this to yourself. Mika's already gone. I don't say that to be insensitive…it's just…at this point, she's no longer suffering. For her sake, I hope she didn't endure excruciating pain. But what you're doing to yourself… You're re-creating that pain every day. Your suffering is continuing."

Omar squeezed his eyes shut. He knew that Gabrielle was right. There were times he told himself the very same thing.

The biggest reality of all was that he couldn't take back what had already happened, no matter how many times he thought about it. All he could pray was that Mika was resting in peace.

"I feel guilty," he said. "All the time."

Suddenly, Gabrielle was turning in her seat. She stroked his face gently and said softly, "I'm so sorry you went through that. But don't blame yourself. Don't give yourself that kind of guilt for the rest of your life."

"No matter how insignificant you think what happened today was, I know firsthand that an unstable person can strike when you least expect it. So please, will you go inside and talk to the detective? It's better to have this incident on record. Besides…if you have a description of the car, it might actually help lead to the arsonist."

Gabrielle's eyes lit up. He saw in her expression that she hadn't considered that aspect before—that she might have another clue to the arsonist's identity.

"Okay," Gabrielle said. "Let's go."

Chapter 21

It took five minutes before the detective came out to greet them. And when she did, Gabrielle's stomach sank.

"Hey, stranger," the woman said, and opened her arms to Omar for a hug. He obliged. "I haven't heard back from you. Why are you being so elusive?"

Omar gestured toward Gabrielle. "Kelly, this is Gabrielle. She's the one I called you about. Gabrielle, this is Kelly Knight, a detective who's working the case of the arsonist."

The woman leveled a bright smile on her, but Gabrielle also saw the suspicion in her eyes. Kelly was beautiful. Her hair was pulled back, completely revealing her face. She had bright eyes, dimples. A medium complexion. But something about her made Gabrielle's gut constrict.

Oh, my God, she thought, reality hitting her. Omar had slept with this woman!

"Cable Four, *Your Hour*," Kelly said. "I watch your show all the time."

Gabrielle smiled tightly. "Thank you."

"Why don't we head into my office and you can tell me what's going on," Kelly said.

Once in Kelly's office, Gabrielle was more convinced than ever that Omar had slept with her. It was the way she looked at him. Gabrielle could read it in the woman's eyes.

"Tell me what happened," Kelly said.

So Gabrielle did. She told her about the newscast, how they had dedicated the whole show to catching the arsonist.

"I thought it was a bad idea the first time she did it," Omar said. "I think what happened today was no coincidence."

"Did you get a look at the car?" Kelly asked.

"It was black," Gabrielle said. "Maybe a Ford. Or a Kia. I'm not exactly sure. Once I thought it was following me, I tried losing it."

"And did you get a license plate?" Kelly asked.

"I wish," Gabrielle said. "Again, I was more concerned with trying to lose him. I was so grateful when I was able to drive into the parking lot of the police station."

"And I suppose you didn't get a look at the driver?"

Gabrielle shook her head. "God, I feel stupid. I just… it happened so fast."

Omar suddenly stood. "I'll be back. I'm heading to the restroom."

Once he was out of the office, Kelly asked, "Anything else you can tell me that you think will be helpful?"

"I think the car had a tint," Gabrielle said. "It was kind of compact, from what I could tell. But I definitely think it had four doors. I'm sorry. I wish I had more."

Kelly finished jotting notes and put down her pen. "If this is the arsonist, we have an idea of what kind of car he drives now. It will help us when looking at video footage in the neighborhood of each of the fires."

"Oh," Gabrielle said, hopeful. "That's a great idea."

"So," Kelly began, "are you and Omar involved?"

Gabrielle was caught off guard. "Excuse me?"

"He's got this way of making you feel so special. Like you're the only one in the world."

Gabrielle's stomach sank. She couldn't speak.

"Next thing you know, you're head over heels. And you find out that he never saw you as more than a plaything."

"Why are you—"

"Why am I saying this? Because I think that women should stick together. Warn each other about the players."

Gabrielle felt sick.

"Oh, I'm sorry," Kelly suddenly said. "You're in love with him, aren't you?"

"What you're saying is completely out of line," Gabrielle managed. "You don't know what Omar and I have."

"Has he told you he loves you?" Kelly asked.

The question hit her like a slap in the face.

Kelly obviously took her silence as affirmation. "I know. That's how he gets you."

Gabrielle pushed her chair back and stood. She bolted out of the office.

She saw Omar heading down the hallway as she was on her way out. "Gabby," he called to her.

Gabrielle quickly headed toward the exit.

"Gabby, what are you doing?"

Gabrielle made a dash for the door. When she got outside, she sprinted to her car.

Omar caught up to her at her car door. "What on earth is going on?" he demanded.

"Why would you bring me to a woman you slept with?" Gabrielle asked.

"She told you that?"

"She didn't have to. It was obvious."

Omar's eyes narrowed. "Kelly and I had a brief fling. It doesn't affect—"

Gabrielle guffawed. "You're unbelievable."

She turned to open the car door, but Omar whirled her around. "Why are you taking off?"

"You made me think you weren't a player. But you have left so many women brokenhearted."

"Is that what Kelly told you?" Omar asked.

"She gave me a heads-up—woman to woman."

"You have got to be kidding me."

Gabrielle felt like an idiot. This past month with Omar had been incredible. So incredible she'd started to believe…

"You haven't said that you love me," Gabrielle blurted out.

Omar looked confused. "You haven't said it, either."

She hadn't said it because she'd been afraid to. Afraid that he didn't love her back. So she'd tried to live in the moment, go with the flow.

"I'm leaving," Gabrielle said.

"Damn it, Gabby. Why?"

"Because…" She stopped, emotion threatening to overwhelm her. "Because all good things come to an end. I knew from the beginning that this relationship had an expiration date."

"You're breaking up with me?"

"Did we even have a relationship?" Gabrielle countered. "Or just an arrangement?"

"I thought we had a relationship."

Gabrielle shook her head. What Kelly had said echoed what she'd heard from her friend about Omar. He had a lot of women, and left them all brokenhearted. He might be into her for a while, but at some point, he would move on.

"Guys like you...you don't do relationships."

Omar's eyes flashed with fire. He pinned her body against her car door with his. "I don't do relationships? Or *you* don't? Because you're the one who's running."

"Because I'm not stupid. I always knew... Look, let's just cut our losses and move on."

"Cut our losses?"

"Omar, you and I both know that whatever this is, it wasn't going to last forever. It was sexual," Gabrielle added, not sure why she was saying that. For her, it had been more than sexual. But she couldn't allow herself to be vulnerable any longer. Omar might be into her for now, but how long would that interest last?

Tobias had proposed. And had slept with her cousin anyway.

"When I think about it," Gabrielle went on, "we spent most of the time having sex."

His eyebrows shot up. "Now you're complaining? You weren't complaining the last time we were together."

Despite the situation, Gabrielle felt a rush of heat. Sex had clouded things for her. Omar was so good in bed. It was as Pauline had said. The more she had sex with Omar, the more likely she'd be to develop feelings for him.

"Omar, you know—"

Omar kissed her. And God, for that moment, Gabrielle was lost. But her heart began to ache, and Gabrielle pushed him away.

"I love you," Omar rasped.

"Now that your old girlfriend has spoken to me you tell me you love me? I...I don't believe you."

Omar flinched, as though she'd hit him. "Wow."

"Omar, it's over," Gabrielle quickly went on. "Everything has an expiration date, and…ours is today."

"So, that's just it?" Omar asked.

Gabrielle steeled her jaw. She couldn't back down. Her feelings for Omar were so strong, she knew that he had the power to totally crush her heart in the future.

So she said, "That's just it."

Omar stalked around to the driver's side of his vehicle, and she flinched when she heard his car door slam shut. A few seconds after that, his tires were squealing as he backed out of the parking spot.

Only when Omar's SUV tore off down State Street did Gabrielle get into her car. She rested her head against the steering wheel and started to cry.

Omar was livid.

One minute, he'd been happily involved with Gabrielle. The next, he'd been dumped.

All because of something Kelly had said to her?

Omar had almost marched back into the police station to confront Kelly, but knew that he was too upset to do so without causing a scene. So he waited until he got home.

He called Kelly's cell.

She answered right away, "Hey, stranger."

Her upbeat tone ticked him off even more. "What did you say to Gabrielle?" he demanded.

For a moment, Kelly said nothing. Then she said, "She's not your type, Omar."

Omar's anger grew. "What did you say to her?"

"Omar, you're not the kind of guy who settles down. You and I both know that. And I'm okay with that. You shouldn't string someone along who's actually into you."

What was it with some of the women Omar had gotten involved with? No wonder he had never forged real relationships with any of them. In his gut, he'd known that they weren't right for him.

"So you're refusing to answer my question? You cross the line and get involved in my business and you think you won't have to answer to that?"

"Look, Omar," Kelly began, her tone softer. "I've missed you, okay? I've called you, tried to schedule time with you, and you've ignored me. All right…maybe I was a little jealous when I saw your new girlfriend. It's just… I always thought we'd end up…you know?"

He didn't know. He hadn't been involved with her in almost a year, and now she was coming up with this?

"Kelly, never talk to me again," Omar said. "Don't call, don't text. If we have to talk to each other because of work, so be it. But other than that, forget you ever knew me."

"Omar—"

He hung up.

Then he started to punch in Gabrielle's number—but stopped.

I love you.

I—I don't believe you.

Omar felt a piercing pain in his gut as he relived that awful moment with Gabrielle. He'd told her that he loved her, and she'd shot him down without missing a beat.

He could see her being upset by whatever Kelly had said. Kelly had had no right to speak to her about anything other than the case. But to simply dismiss him and his feelings, what they'd shared… Didn't she know how he felt?

The added insult was that she'd had the nerve to blame him for ending things, when it was obvious to Omar that she had been looking for the first opportunity to bail.

At the very least, she owed it to him to talk to him.

Instead, she'd simply cut him out of her life. And she'd all but called him a player incapable of forging a lasting relationship.

Omar went to the fridge and got himself a beer, then slumped onto the sofa again. He took a long drink from the bottle, then glanced around his massive living room. He'd lived alone here for years and had been happy that way. Now, when he looked around, he saw Gabrielle everywhere. This house wasn't the same without her presence.

The two of them cooking in his chef's kitchen.

The two of them cuddling on the sofa in his entertainment room, watching a movie.

The two of them making love.

On the bed. On the floor. In the shower.

Yeah, they'd had a lot of sex. Because they'd both been unable to keep their hands off each other. Omar saw nothing wrong with that. In fact, it was amazing to have a woman who stoked his desire to such a degree, while also filling his heart with happiness.

They certainly hadn't only spent their time making love. He had been by her side for the several hours it took for her father's triple bypass surgery to be completed. They talked. A lot. And he'd finally told her about his past with Mika—something he'd never told anyone else. He resented the implication that he was only using her for sex.

After fifteen years, Omar had finally fallen in love again.

But if Gabrielle couldn't trust him, couldn't believe him… Then he had no choice but to do what she'd said they should do.

Cut his losses and move on.

Chapter 22

Gabrielle was glad that the next day was a Saturday, because she was in no mood to get out of bed. She kept wondering why, if she'd done the right thing with Omar, did she feel so awful.

I love you.

I don't believe you.

Gabrielle's gut contorted as she recalled what she'd said to him when he'd proclaimed his feelings. Had she really told him that she didn't believe him? Finally, he'd told her that he loved her, words she had longed to hear... And she had completely dismissed them.

Gabrielle had just been so stunned by that officer talking to her about Omar. And yes, she'd let Kelly's comments get to her. But it wasn't really Kelly who was the problem. Kelly's unsolicited opinion had brought all of Gabrielle's fears to the forefront.

And her biggest fear was that what she had with Omar wouldn't last.

I love you.

Gabrielle was too afraid to believe his proclamation. Afraid that she would end up more heartbroken than she had ever been in her life. Because she loved Omar more than she'd ever loved anyone else.

The men she'd dated had claimed to love her...only to betray her in some way. Tobias hadn't been the first, but Gabrielle had vowed that he would be the last. She'd honestly believed that Tobias, being sophisticated, professional and generally more mature than the men she'd dated before, would be the partner she had longed for. But despite their engagement, Tobias had betrayed her just like the other men in her life had before him.

Gabrielle had been wrecked. She'd had to take three days off work after that. And as Pauline had so aptly put it, she'd been in a funk ever since.

Until Omar. Omar had made her come alive. He'd made he feel hopeful and happy again.

And yet she knew, without doubt, that if things got even more serious with Omar, and he ended up leaving her...

Well, she wasn't sure she would recover.

So she'd done what she'd had to do. Ending things now was the only way to ensure that she could spare herself further pain.

Yet she was in a whole world of pain right now.

Gabrielle called Pauline. "Can we get together?" she asked after Pauline greeted her.

"You okay?" Pauline asked.

"No," Gabrielle admitted, her voice whimpering. "I'm not."

"I was just about to head out and get something to eat," Pauline said. "Maybe you can join me?"

Gabrielle didn't particularly want to get out of bed, but maybe getting out of bed would do her good.

"All right," Gabrielle said. "Our favorite Mexican spot?"

"Actually, how about that Asian restaurant, Greens? It's a vegan restaurant."

"A new diet?"

"No," Pauline said. "Haven't you noticed? None of the vegan restaurants have been firebombed."

Gabrielle felt an odd sensation at Pauline's statement. The kind of sensation she had when something in her mind suddenly clicked.

"Oh, my God, Pauline," Gabrielle said. "You're right. No vegan establishments have been attacked. Not that there are many of them in town, but…" Her brain scrambled to connect the dots that suddenly seemed obvious. "My parents had a steakhouse. And all the other restaurants set on fire served meat." She perked up. "And, oh, my goodness, a meat packaging company was set on fire. It suddenly all makes sense."

"You're thinking…" Pauline began. "You're thinking the arsonist is some sort of animal activist?"

"What you just said…it's like fitting a piece in a puzzle."

"And I don't even know why I said that. I guess subconsciously I made the connection."

"Pauline, you're a genius!"

"Has that ever been in doubt?"

"I'm going to have to call you back," Gabrielle suddenly said.

"What about—"

"You go get that bite to eat. I'll talk to you later."

Gabrielle ended the call and dialed Omar's number. In

her gut, she believed she had the one clue that could lead to the arsonist's identity.

He didn't answer, so she left him a message.

"Omar, I just learned something that can really narrow down the list of suspects. In fact, I think this is the break the city needs. Call me back as soon as possible."

Then Gabrielle hung up the phone, hoping Omar would get back to her soon.

Gabrielle waited. And waited. And as Saturday evening rolled around, Omar had not returned her call.

By noon on Sunday, he still hadn't called. Nor texted.

And with each hour that passed, Gabrielle felt worse and worse. Because she'd had nothing but time to think about what she'd done.

I love you.

I don't believe you.

The expression on Omar's face when she'd said that... it was as if she'd slapped him. Gabrielle had been angry because of what Kelly had said to her. But mostly, she'd been scared. So much so that she hadn't wanted to accept Omar's proclamation as the truth. But the look in his eyes matched what her heart believed.

He *did* love her. Just as she loved him.

She'd felt that love every time they'd been intimate. When they'd talked. And when he'd stayed with her for the entire duration of her father's surgery.

"Oh, God," she whimpered. What had she done?

She'd thrown away the best thing that had happened to her...*ever*. All because she had been afraid to feel any pain. Instead, she'd caused Omar pain. She'd seen it in his eyes, and continued to see it as she replayed that awful scene outside the police station in her mind.

Gabrielle got dressed. She had to see Omar and make things right.

As she drove to his house a short while later, she only hoped that he was home.

Anxiety filled every fiber of Gabrielle's being as she turned into Omar's driveway. His car was there.

He was home.

Suddenly, she was afraid to go to his door. Because this moment would determine her future. Absolutely everything was on the line right now. Omar could tell her that he never wanted to see her again. Or, he could hear her out and allow her to explain why she'd pushed him away.

It had only been two days without him, and already Gabrielle missed him terribly. Thinking that cutting him out of her life to spare herself future pain suddenly seemed like an insane idea.

Gabrielle's heart pounded as she exited her car and walked to Omar's front door. She raised her finger to the doorbell, but didn't press it.

Just do it, she told herself.

She pressed it, and heard the chiming sound going off in the house. It seemed as if several minutes passed before she saw Omar's form approaching behind the tempered glass doors.

She watched as Omar stood there, not opening the door. Was he going to leave her standing there?

Finally, he swung the door open. He looked at Gabrielle in confusion.

Gabrielle drew in a deep breath. "Hey."

"What are you doing here?" Omar asked, his tone neutral.

"Did you…did you get my message?"

A beat. "Yeah. I did."

"Omar, I think I have a serious lead where the arsonist is concerned. I was excited to share it with you. I thought you'd—"

"Did you call Kelly?" he asked.

"No—"

"Any leads you have regarding the case, call her. Or another officer if you'd rather speak to someone else."

"I…" Gabrielle swallowed. "I was hoping we could talk."

"Why?"

"Because I know I didn't handle the situation on Friday the best way."

"The *situation*?" Omar looked aghast. "You basically called me a liar and dumped me. Then you call me the next day to consult about the damn arsonist?"

"I called you because…because you were the first person I wanted to share this news with."

"You've got to be kidding me," Omar said.

"I don't mean it that way. You were the first person I wanted to call—don't you get it? Because I wanted to hear your voice. I wanted to share this news with you the way I've shared other things with you. What I said to you on Friday, I shouldn't have said. If I could take it back, I would. I had a knee-jerk reaction, and I feel awful about that. Please, can I just come in so we can talk?"

"Do you think you're the only one who's ever been hurt?" Omar asked. "Or do you think I'm incapable of feeling any emotion?"

His questions silenced her. She didn't know how to respond.

"That's what I thought," he said.

"No," she quickly said. "Of course I don't think you're incapable of emotion. It's just that I—"

"*I,*" Omar interjected. "That's the problem, Gabby.

Two people exist in a relationship. Not just one. But you made a decision for both of us as if you're the only one with any vested interest here."

"You're right. And that's why I'm here. I'm sorry—"

"I told you I loved you. And you said you didn't believe me."

The weight of that statement hung between them, like a physical barrier.

"Omar, I'm sorry. What I said, it was awful. Absolutely inexcusable." Gabrielle looked up at him, her eyes imploring him to hear her out. "I know an apology's lame—"

"I could understand you being upset by what Kelly said. She was out of line—and I made that clear when I talked to her. But for you to completely shut me out, to ignore me altogether, to tell me I was *lying*… You started off not trusting my character when we first met, and it's pretty clear that opinion never changed."

Tears filled Gabrielle's eyes. "No, you're wrong. That was my fear talking."

"I can't do this, Gabby," he said.

"Please, Omar. Let's just talk."

"You told me to move on," he said. "I'm taking your advice."

"No—"

He closed the door. For a long moment he stood there, then walked away.

Gabrielle's breath came in quick gasps. She waited, hoping that any second Omar would come back to the door.

But he didn't.

After five minutes, Gabrielle turned and headed to her car, her heart breaking.

And it was her own fault.

Chapter 23

Somehow, Gabrielle managed to drive out of Omar's neighborhood without wrecking her car. An incredible feat, considering how distressed she was.

She drove across town to Pauline's place, and was relieved when she found her best friend home. If ever she'd needed Pauline, it was now.

Fifteen minutes after entering Pauline's townhouse, Gabrielle was curled on one side of her sofa, a glass of sangria in her hand. "I know I was harsh," Gabrielle said, her voice ripe with emotion, "but he wouldn't even let me explain? Not even after I said I was sorry?"

"What did you expect?" Pauline asked her.

"I expected him to…to try and understand."

"You called him because you wanted to talk about the arsonist. That doesn't scream, *I want to talk to you about us.*"

"I called him because I wanted to share the theory with him."

"You have to see how it looks from his perspective."

Gabrielle sipped her drink. "I know. I guess in some way, I thought that talking about the arsonist was a way to break the ice."

"And he saw you as having a single-minded focus. Catching the arsonist."

"But I also apologized."

"You also told Omar that you didn't believe him." Pauline frowned as she looked Gabrielle in the eye. "Girl, a man lays his heart on the line like that and you shoot him down? You know that's not cool."

Gabrielle whimpered, then wiped at her eyes. "I'd just had some woman he slept with warning me not to fall for him."

"Which you didn't see as strange?" Pauline asked. "A little wacko? I mean, who does that?"

Gabrielle covered her face with a hand. "I didn't think."

"You messed up. Big time. What Omar said about a relationship being about two people, he's absolutely right."

"I get it. For a moment, I was paralyzed with fear, and I pushed him away out of fear."

"No," Pauline countered. "You brought out your inner control freak—who can be really cold, by the way. You didn't want to be vulnerable. You wanted to control your relationship with Omar instead of letting yourself fall without a safety net. And that's not how it works, Gabby. You can't control love."

Gabrielle sipped more of her sangria. She wished there was a dark hole in the ground where she could stay until this pain passed.

"All I wanted was the chance to talk to him."

"And now he's doing what you were doing," Pauline said. "Trying to protect himself from pain." Pauline shifted on the sofa to fully face Gabrielle. "Can I speak frankly?"

"Why do I get the feeling I'm not going to like this?"

"Because you're not." Pauline put her sangria glass down on the table, then crossed her legs on the sofa and folded her hands in her lap. "The cause of everything that has gone wrong in your life—well, almost everything— is your need to control everything."

"I've been hurt. I've been betrayed. Is it so wrong to want to protect myself?"

"But that's not how life works. You don't get to control if you fall in love, or who falls in love with you. And you want some even harsher truth?"

Gabrielle's chest tightened. "Fine. Have at it."

"You pushed Tobias away."

The words hit Gabrielle like a cold glass of water being thrown in her face. She was stunned and crushed at the words that had left her friend's mouth.

"I can't believe you'd say that."

"I'm not saying that he doesn't bear any responsibility for what happened. But you set him up. You tried to control the situation—and you set him up for failure."

"If he loved me—"

"He would not have responded to your cousin's advances? Maybe so. But there were extenuating circumstances. You sent Jessica in there, you had her try to seduce Tobias and she clearly did a great job. He's human." Pauline quickly held up a hand when Gabrielle opened her mouth to protest. "I'm not saying that what he did was excusable. Just that maybe you shouldn't have been so stunned to learn that he failed your ridiculous test."

"He didn't just sleep with Jessica. He moved in with her. He—he humiliated me!"

"So is that what this is about? The fact that you were humiliated?"

Gabrielle said nothing.

"And maybe the truth is that you sensed something between Jessica and Tobias, that's why you even had her do the job." Pauline shrugged. "I don't know. All I know, is that instead of trusting him, you pushed him into the arms of another woman. And when he failed, you blamed him. I don't know what you were like dealing with him day-to-day, but maybe he figured out that you didn't completely trust him. Maybe your level of needing to control everything got to him."

Tears streamed down Gabrielle's face. "You're supposed to be in my corner," she said.

"And I am," Pauline said softly. "That's why I'm telling you this. I don't want to see you blow something else because you've got to control every aspect of it."

Pauline's words were like a hammer, pounding in the truth. Omar had told her that he loved her, and Gabrielle's first reaction had been disbelief. Why?

The answer came to her instantly and clearly. She'd been hurt so many times before. No matter how wonderfully the relationship had started, she was always waiting for the other shoe to drop. She expected it to fail.

To have an expiration date.

All good things come to an end. I knew from the beginning that this relationship had an expiration date.

Kelly's words had been the catalyst for sending Gabrielle into self-preservation mode. Her response had been automatic. Unemotional.

Efficient.

She hadn't allowed herself any vulnerability, because in that moment, she'd only been thinking of protecting herself from pain. She hadn't even been willing to hear Omar out.

How could she blame him for now not wanting to give her a moment to explain?

Gabrielle gasped softly. "Oh, God." She threw her hand to her mouth to stifle her sobs as she thought about everything Pauline had said—and how her own behavior had negatively affected her life. "I did push Tobias away. I don't know if he would have cheated eventually, but I made it easy for him. Maybe you're right. Deep down in his heart, Tobias realized that I didn't trust him. And now Omar... I always think they're gonna leave. So I..."

"Push them away first," Pauline finished for her.

Gabrielle looked at her friend through tear-filled eyes. Pauline was right. She was absolutely right.

"But what I said to Omar..."

"Can't be unsaid. But you can make him hear you. Make him believe you. If you're not afraid, and you're willing to put your heart on the line... Willing to relinquish control... I think you can salvage things." Pauline shrugged. "And if he doesn't...maybe he isn't the guy for you."

Gabrielle thought about their lovemaking. How intense and beautiful and meaningful it had felt to her. Had it actually felt the same way to him?

"If he doesn't believe me," Gabrielle said, shaking her head, "I can't blame him. I did this. I...I hurt him as surely as if I took a knife and cut out his heart."

"So you're giving up?" Pauline asked.

"No," Gabrielle said. "I'm going to fight for him. Someway, somehow, I'm going to fight for him."

And to do that, Gabrielle was going to have to let herself be totally vulnerable. She was going to have to risk the greatest pain in the world, in order to attain the greatest happiness.

Chapter 24

The next morning, although Gabrielle didn't have any interest in talking to Kelly, she did her due diligence and called her to share her theory that the arsonist might be an animal rights activist. And when Gabrielle shared that theory with Janine, Janine's eyes filled with excitement.

"I need you to run that story on *Your Hour* today," Janine said. "This feels right. It feels like the missing piece to the puzzle."

Gabrielle wished she could have talked to Omar about this, get his opinion. But she knew the last thing he'd want to hear out of her mouth was any more talk about the arsonist. No, the next time they spoke, it had to be about them.

She wasn't sure yet how to get through to him, but she was determined to figure out a way. Because she wasn't going to let Omar go without a fight.

Not a chance.

*   *   *

Every news outlet ran with the theory that the arsonist was likely an animal rights activist. The pictures Gabrielle had taken, along with her general description of the man and the car she believed that he drove, dominated the news over the next few days.

And on Wednesday, Gabrielle got the call that changed everything.

"There's a caller on line three," Renée said to Gabrielle on the other end of the phone. "She said she has to talk to you and only you."

Gabrielle clicked to answer that extension. "Gabrielle Leonard."

"Gabrielle, hi. My name is Amy. I'm calling…well, I saw your shows and all the news broadcasts and I think… I think I know who the arsonist is. Actually, I'm pretty sure that he's my boyfriend."

Gabrielle listened as the woman spoke about her boyfriend, an angry animal rights activist who believed that the citizens of Ocean City needed to be held accountable for consuming meat and contributing to the suffering of animals.

"He lost his dad last year," Amy explained, "and everything spiraled out of control for him."

"Why do you believe he's the arsonist?" Gabrielle asked.

"The night of every fire, he wasn't here. A couple of times, I could smell gasoline on his clothes. And after the last fire, he had an unexplained burn on his hand. He didn't want to go to the hospital."

Gabrielle's stomach fluttered and her skin tingled. *This is it…* "Amy, you have to go to the police with this."

"I'm scared," Amy said.

"Where's your boyfriend now?"

"At work."

"Don't be scared. If you can do it now, I'll go to the police with you."

"He's a good person. He's just…he's just lost his way."

Gabrielle spoke gently. "It sounds like he's had a tough time. I know what that's like. I… I almost lost my dad after his restaurant was burned down. He had a heart attack and almost died." She paused. "The very fact that you're calling me tells me that you don't want to see anyone else hurt."

"I don't. God knows, I don't."

"Then meet me here at Cable Four. I'll go to the police station with you."

The next day, when Gabrielle walked into the Cable Four building, she stopped in her tracks. Everyone she worked with was standing in the waiting area off the entrance, and they all began to applaud. The station manager, the camera operators, the assistants. Renée. Everyone clapped and cheered.

"Well done!" Fred, one of the cameramen, said. He raised his hands high and began to cheer loudly, inspiring everyone to ramp up the applause again.

Janine walked over to her and hugged her. "I can't believe Cable Four has its very own hero. Our Gabrielle Leonard single-handedly cracked the arsonist case."

"Hear, hear!" someone said.

Gabrielle smiled bashfully. When she'd heard the news of the arrest this morning, she'd been over the moon. And the first person she'd wanted to call had been Omar.

"I'm not the one who solved the case," Gabrielle said. "Amy Cummins deserves all the credit. She's the one who realized that she was living with the arsonist."

"Yeah, but you helped tighten the rein," Sterling said.

He was one of the assistants. "The guy made mistakes, and without your pressure, we might still have an arsonist out there terrorizing our city."

Gabrielle beamed. It felt good knowing that this crazy person had finally been apprehended.

Obviously, he was deranged. Gabrielle could understand that he cared about animal suffering and wanted to bring attention to the cause. But he had hurt people and devastated lives in the process. And he'd been responsible for the death of firefighter Dean Dunbar.

"I'm just so glad that the police acted swiftly in the investigation," Gabrielle said.

"Can you believe that idiot had a storage unit filled with his arson supplies?" Renée asked.

"Criminals are notoriously dumb," Fred stated.

"He was downright nuts," Janine said. "And talk about the wrong way to get a message across. There are a lot of amazing vegan restaurants, and I enjoy going to them. Thank God he's off the streets. That is one huge relief."

"Yes, thank God," Gabrielle said.

"Let's hear it for Gabrielle!" Janine whooped and started to clap.

There was another exuberant round of applause, and Gabrielle bowed. She felt a wave of elation as it hit her anew that the arsonist, Sebastian Franic, had actually been apprehended.

The next instant, her elation was tempered with a measure of sadness. All she wanted to do was call Omar.

She wanted to share this moment with him.

But he wasn't even talking to her.

"And the book again is *Onward and Upward: A Practical Guide for Moving on After Divorce*, by Sharon Bluestone." Gabrielle turned toward Sharon and offered her a smile. "Thank you so much for coming in today."

"You're welcome."

Gabrielle faced the camera. On the teleprompter were the words she was supposed to read for the closing of the show. She was supposed to close by reiterating the arrest of the arsonist, and the relief the city was feeling. But Gabrielle was suddenly inspired to go off script.

"For everybody watching, I have something to say. And I hope you'll bear with me. I suppose my talk with Sharon about moving on after a relationship has made it clear to me that there's something I need to do right now. Sharon so eloquently talked about knowing when you need to move on, and when you need to fight. And right now, I need to fight."

Gabrielle saw the confused look on Fred's face as he was behind the camera, but she continued, undeterred.

"I was recently in a relationship. I fell for this guy, and I fell hard. In part because I fell so hard, I was also terrified. Love can do that to you. Make you incredibly happy, but also incredibly afraid. And I was afraid that this relationship wouldn't last.

"Now I know that some of you are confused. I never talk about my private life like this. But sometimes you have to publicly make a wrong, right. And that's what I'm doing now. Because I did everything in my power to push this person away. I really hope you're watching right now. Because I want to tell you again just how sorry I am. I was afraid to open up my heart because I was afraid of being hurt. But over these days since we've been apart, I've learned that I can't control everything. And that's actually the beauty of life. The surprises you don't expect. Those surprises can be so incredible…if you aren't your own worst enemy.

"And that's exactly what I was. My own worst enemy. And I hurt you in the process. And while I don't deserve your forgiveness, I'm hoping that you *will* forgive me. I'm hoping that you'll realize that what I'm saying right now means something. And it means that I've taken a good hard look at myself... At what we had... And I don't want to lose it."

Gabrielle felt emotion filling her chest, and she did her best to keep her composure. But even still, as she began to speak again, her voice cracked slightly. "Omar... Yes, I'm saying your name. I love you. And I'm not afraid anymore. Because I know that love is worth every risk. And even if you don't feel the same way, I don't regret what we shared. I only regret that I was so blind I couldn't see the truth."

She smiled for the camera again, then said brightly, "I'm Gabrielle Leonard, and this has been *Your Hour*. Thanks so much for tuning in today."

Omar stood in front of the TV in the lounge area, his heart thumping wildly. You could hear a pin drop in the firehouse. Everyone was watching and listening to Gabrielle as she laid her heart bare, with all the citizens of Ocean City as her witnesses.

Omar was riveted. He was mystified. Was Gabrielle actually on live television, speaking to the entire viewing audience about *him*?

About them?

I love you. And I'm not afraid anymore. Because I know that love is worth every risk.

His eyes held hers through the screen, and it was suddenly as though it were only the two of them alone in a room. And she was telling him what was in her heart.

Suddenly, Mason was approaching him. He clamped

a hand down on Omar's shoulder. "Now I know who the special lady is," Mason said. "And now I know why you've been sulking during the past two shifts."

A slow breath oozed out of Omar's chest. "You heard that, right? I wasn't imagining it."

"Nope," Mason said.

A smile crept onto Omar's lips. "If you know her...for her to do this with all of Ocean City watching..."

"Can I ask you something?" Mason said.

"Sure, man. Anything."

"Why are you still standing here?"

Omar faced him with a huge grin, then turned and headed out the door toward the bay where the trucks were.

He went directly to the fire truck.

"No one drives that truck but me," Tyler said.

"I'm not about to miss this," Mason said.

"Me neither," another man said.

"Suit up," Mason said. "In case we get a call."

And the next thing Omar knew, Omar's brothers were suiting up and getting into both the engine and ladder trucks. It was as if they were all heading out to an emergency call.

And he supposed, in a way, they were.

At the cable station, Tyler gave the siren a blast. Then Omar hopped out of the truck.

Someone from inside the station came to the front window and looked out. Then she turned quickly. Omar recognized her as the receptionist. By the time he was heading into the front door, he saw Gabrielle coming out into the foyer.

Her lips parted as she looked at him. A world of emotions flashed on her face.

"You saw?" she asked.

He stalked toward her. "Yes."

Confusion flashed in her eyes. She was unsure. Vulnerable.

"Of all the crazy stunts," Omar said.

"I don't know what came over me," Gabrielle said. "I just…suddenly I knew that I needed to do it. Needed to make you understand." She kept her gaze locked on his as she continued. "I know you may never forgive me…"

In the past, she would have glanced away. Made herself less vulnerable. But now, she looked up at him, her face softening. Her fear was palpable, yet she wasn't shying away from it.

She was facing it.

"How could I not forgive you?" he asked.

Her chest heaved with a heavy breath. "You do?"

"Yes."

"I was so awful to you. When I think about what I said, I just—"

Omar slipped an arm around her waist. "It's okay, baby," he whispered.

Tears filled Gabrielle's eyes. "I'm sorry."

"I know."

"I never meant—"

He silenced her with a kiss. Because a week without her in his life had been entirely too long. And all he wanted to do was feel her soft lips beneath his, hear the soft sounds she made as she surrendered to his touch.

A sob escaping from her lips, Gabrielle slipped her arms around his neck and kissed him back. And as her body and lips melted against his, the sweetest feelings of love and hope filled Omar's heart.

He broke the kiss and whispered, "Kissing you is the best way I know to shut you up."

Tears streaming down her face, she chuckled. Omar wiped her tears with the pads of his thumbs.

"I know how scary it is to let down your guard," Omar went on. "Baby, I get it. I never thought I'd be able to open my heart to love again, either. Not after what happened to Mika. But I've finally met the woman I know I want to be with forever."

"Oh, Omar." Gabrielle whimpered. "I didn't expect you. I didn't expect to fall in love. Not now." She paused. "I used to hate the unexpected. But now I know…now I know that the unexpected is one of life's most wonderful gifts. You're the man I love, and you were totally unexpected. But you're oh so spectacular."

"You're spectacular," Omar said softly. "And I want to marry you."

Gabrielle gasped. So did the receptionist.

Omar looked into Gabrielle's eyes. He wasn't sure what had come over him. But he knew—without doubt—that it was right.

No, that wasn't true. He knew exactly what had come over him. Love.

"I want to marry you," he repeated, truly owning the words this time. "What do you say, baby? Will you be my wife?"

"Are you serious?"

"I've never been more serious about anything in my life."

Squealing, Gabrielle threw her arms around his neck and kissed him deeply.

"Is that a yes?" Omar asked when she broke the kiss.

"Yes!" Gabrielle exclaimed.

Omar scooped her into his arms and whirled her around. He heard the applause before he saw the audience of staff members from the cable station.

Then he carried a giggling Gabrielle out the front

door to where his fellow firefighters stood in front of the trucks, clearly taking in the show.

"She said yes!" Omar announced. And his brothers began to hoot, holler and cheer.

Omar looked at Gabrielle. The smile on her face was more radiant than he had ever seen.

"I'll get you a ring as soon as—"

"Shut up and kiss me," she commanded, tugging on his collar.

So he did.

And as his mouth met hers, a feeling of overwhelming bliss filled his heart and soul.

It was nothing he had ever experienced before. And it was all because of the incredible woman he held in his arms.

"I love you," Gabrielle whispered.

"I love you, too, baby. So much."

Omar had finally met the woman who intrigued him in every way. And the fact that she loved him back?

Well, that made him the luckiest man in the world.

* * * * *

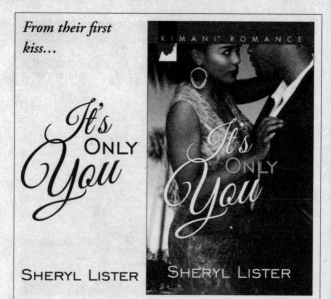

REQUEST YOUR FREE BOOKS!

2 FREE NOVELS PLUS 2 FREE GIFTS!

KIMANI™ ROMANCE

Love's ultimate destination!

This summer is going to be hot, hot, hot
with a new miniseries
from fan-favorite authors!

YAHRAH ST. JOHN
LISA MARIE PERRY
PAMELA YAYE

HEAT WAVE OF DESIRE

Available June 2015

HOT SUMMER NIGHTS

Available July 2015

HEAT OF PASSION

Available August 2015

California Desert Dreams

www.Harlequin.com